In **Part 1**, Cyril ~~~~ evil plot that c~~~~ plague. With the b~~~~ Minister, Cyril and his trusted cohort, Geoffrey Cowlishaw, travel to the coast of England. There they meet Letchworth, the sea captain who will take them to Italy. . .to a top-secret meeting with Pope Adolfo I. Aboard Letchworth's ship, Cyril and Geoffrey make some amazing discoveries and witness a dramatic self-sacrifice.

*Now, Roger Elwood's
riveting six-part adventure
continues with. . .*

PART 2
VALLEY OF THE SHADOW

Roger Elwood, whose gripping suspense titles have occupied best-seller lists over the past ten years, is well known to readers of Christian fiction. Such Elwood page-turners as *Angelwalk*, *Fallen Angel*, *Stedfast*, and *Darien* have together sold more than 400,000 copies.

A RIVETING SIX-PART ADVENTURE

PART 2
WITHOUT THE DAWN

VALLEY OF THE SHADOW

ROGER
ELWOOD

A Barbour Book

© MCMXCVII by Roger Elwood

ISBN 1-57748-039-2

Published by Barbour & Company, Inc.
          P.O. Box 719
          Uhrichsville, Ohio 44683
          http://www.barbourbooks.com

ecpa Member of the
Evangelical Christian
Publishers Association

Printed in the United States of America.

CHAPTER 1

Midway across the English Channel, October 1994. . .

They had no captain now.

Henry Letchworth, the captain's brother, was not in a reasonable condition, mentally or emotionally, and he would have to be carefully watched until they reached the coast of France late the next day. Under normal circumstances, first mate Randall Kirksey would assume command of the ship but he did not feel comfortable in that role just yet.

"I'm but the newest member of the crew and I haven't had enough experience," he said as they gathered in the crew's quarters on the ship's third level, with only the navigator and one sail man left aboveboard. "I know that Captain Letchworth was going to ease me in gradually a year or two from now, which was when he was thinkin' ahead to retirement but he was taken from us and—"

His words choked in his throat.

"However, you *are* first mate, Mr. Kirksey," Geoffrey reminded the other man, after waiting briefly for him to continue speaking. "Despite your admitted youth, you must have had a great deal of ability for the captain to consider appointing you."

"But *he* did not make me first mate, sir," Kirksey confessed, looking ever more uncomfortable. "One of the owners did."

"How in the world did that happen?" Geoffrey asked, realizing how unusual that sort of thing was, in part because of the resentment it had been known to stir among veteran seamen already onboard.

"I am the owner's son. Father thought I was too effete, I suppose. He wanted to toughen me by the sort of experiences I would gain living and working with real men."

Geoffrey expected the other crew members to grumble when reminded of this, as veterans of the sea generally were prone to do when position and influence got a man a job that only hard work and experience should have made possible.

"We did not like our mate Randall here at first, the lot of us here in this crew, we thought he was bein' shoved down our throats," one of them admitted, his cockney accent the heaviest that Cyril and Geoffrey had ever heard. "But Randall done proved what he could do right well. He's fine, this here lad, he is! Captain was pleased with him, which was good enough for us since he would never put anybody to danger for any reason."

Obviously pleased by this, Kirksey shook hands with the man.

"I mean, I know a lot now, and I feel good about myself in the job that I have," Kirksey continued, facing Geoffrey again, "but I think it is too soon for me to become captain of this vessel. It's too big, man! I need another year at sea, maybe more than that."

The crew did something then that was wholly unexpected. As a unit and of the same mind, they turned toward Cyril and Geoffrey and the one with the heavy accent spoke again, this time with great confidence.

"You gentlemen, Lord Fothergill and Lord Cowlishaw, right fine chaps you both are, together you be our captain until we reach land in a day or two, dependin' upon the weather and all. Will you do this for us? We is simple men and we'd sure be honored to serve under you. What could happen between now and then, sirs?"

Wanting to argue, Cyril and Geoffrey instantly gathered into a neat little mental pile all the logical, compelling reasons why they should decline—lack of experience far greater than Kirksey's, possible decisions that could mean life or death for everyone onboard—but they accepted the "appointment" instead, recognizing it as the crew's attempt to honor them, admittedly in deference to their position as lords, but also as testimony to the rapport that had come into being during the extraordinary events of the journey thus far. Throwing it back in their faces seemed a wrongheaded response.

After Cyril thanked the crew and Geoffrey did the same, they started up the steps to their quarters when the sail man who had been on deck came abruptly down toward them, frantic in his manner—he was mindful of the unswerving requirement of not being away from his post longer than necessary—his face wet from the storm, his bloodshot, red-rimmed eyes wide with amazement.

"*Hurry!*" he said, barely able to talk in any coherent manner. "You ain't gonna believe your eyes, sirs."

"What's wrong?" Cyril started to ask but the man had already started back upstairs in considerable haste.

Everyone followed.

Cyril and Geoffrey needed to steady themselves as they saw what had made the sail man act in such a frenzied manner. As each of the crew reached the deck, they, too, staggered and then fought to regain control of their senses.

Captain Letchworth's body. . .

Sprawled in the middle of the deck was the captain's body, scarcely more than an hour after he had been carried from sight by the storm.

Gesticulating wildly, the sail man stood in front of the others.

"I saw everything that happened," he said, his voice

strained. "I saw what they did!"

"Who did this?" Cyril asked.

The man stumbled toward him, forgetting custom, and collapsed into his arms.

"Them whales!" he cried, emotionally overwhelmed. "Them whales did it! Four big ones and that little baby!"

He stepped back, pressing his hands to his cheeks.

"I was fightin' a new gust of wind," he went on, "tryin' to prevent it from wrenchin' the sail ropes from my grip. I happened to be lookin' to that side there, and I saw him bein' flung over the railing. I thought he was alive, his arms movin', his legs!"

He pulled away, unable to endure the sudden stares of his crew mates and turned his back.

"Tell us the rest!" several of them yelled to him. "We love you, mate. You ain't doing nothin' to be ashamed of."

Slowly he faced them again.

"Like a bloody fool, I cried out to him, 'Captain, for the love of God, we thought you were a goner, we thought—' "

Embarrassed and distraught, he was shaking so hard he could not finish.

Cyril walked up to him and whispered, "We're friends, man. We'll not criticize you. Be calm, and tell us the rest as best you can."

"Thank you, sir, thank you for bein' kind," the sail man replied, pausing as he got his thoughts together. "I could hardly wait to tell the rest of you what happened. We were goin' to have our captain back! And through a miracle at that!

"He hit the deck so hard, so very hard, I could almost hear bones acracking all over his body, and then he didn't move, and I then realized what the situation was, playing the part of a fool like I did."

He closed his eyes, trying to steady the images.

"For a moment, I glanced out at the sea, and saw them there, I saw the whales waitin' maybe a couple of minutes, just waitin'. And then they hightailed it away, they did."

A sound behind the group caught their attention.

Henry stood at the top of the steps, staring at his brother's body, his crew mates, and the two passengers to his left. So wobbly that a gust of wind nearly caused him to fall, Henry staggered to that now battered body on the deck.

"Your eyes are open, my dear brother. . ." he muttered, "but they are dead of sight."

He sat down beside Letchworth and gently pressed his eyelids shut, then slid one arm underneath the body while wrapping the other around the chest and hugged that cold, soaked form against him, unmindful of the storm.

"We all need to get below, good friend," Randall Kirksey said after approaching him. "We risk illness if we do not. We'll help you with your brother."

Henry looked up at the first mate and spoke with special dignity, "This is not the brother I love. This is the suit of clothes with which he was adorned for forty years. My brother's gone, not in the sea, but he walks the streets of heaven where I'll be someday, my mind whole. And the two of us'll spend eternity—"

Henry stopped, bowing his head to indicate that he no longer wanted to say anything.

Kirksey nodded as he told the others, "Let's take him below, please, Henry. Will you let your crew mates help you with this?"

"Yes. . ." Henry answered, his voice hardly audible above the continuing noise of a storm that was one of the worst in memory.

Cyril offered to relinquish the quarters he had been as-

signed and Captain Letchworth's body was put in his bed
after being dried, a task that Henry would let no one else per-
form.

A makeshift mattress of thick blankets bundled together
was put on the floor of Geoffrey's room for Cyril. The un-
common images that were swirling around in their minds and
the violent rocking of the ship made it difficult for either man
to fall asleep quickly, but an hour later the storm did start to
lose much of its fury and that motion decreased, the English
Channel becoming less turbulent at last.

CHAPTER 2

After landing at Cherbourg, a seaside town bloated with tourists during the summer season but more like a sleeping maiden during the fall and winter months, Cyril Fothergill and Geoffrey Cowlishaw stayed for a day to help Henry Letchworth and the other crew members prepare for their captain's burial. The two lords would have guessed that it was to have been a funeral at sea but Henry told them that his brother's desire was to be buried on land, that the sea had been a demanding mistress all of his adult life and he had no wish for her to claim him in death.

So it was that Captain Letchworth's body was placed in a grave at the rear of a tiny cemetery on the side of a small hill just inside the town limits of Cherbourg. When Cyril observed that there were not many other graves at that location, first mate Randall Kirksey was quick to explain, "This is a special place, sir, reserved for people who've come to be thought of with an extra degree of respect and affection by the lot of us. Look behind you, sir."

Cyril and Geoffrey turned and saw a long line of men, women, and children from Cherbourg and surrounding communities walking up to the base of the slope and standing there, heads bowed, some wiping tears from their eyes.

The eulogy by Reverend Rupert Evanston, a rather bony-looking, severe-sounding man, was brief but poignant. In closing he said simply, "What finer words could be said of a man, any man than these: 'He was loved.' "

Then each member of the crew stepped forward, one after

the other saying, "He was a hero, my hero," and not for an instant did this seem forced or rehearsed, and not for an instant did it become boring. At the end, the tears that flowed from each man, and from the townspeople a few feet away, were joined by similar expressions of grief from Cyril and Geoffrey, deeply moved by what they saw and heard, each kneeling before the simple coffin and whispering a prayer before they arose, then waiting in silence for the captain's casket to be lowered into the ground.

"Goodbye, dear man," Cyril said before leaving that little cemetery on a hill outside Cherbourg, France. "It was a privilege to have known you. . .friend."

A contingent of five Vatican guards arrived at the prearranged meeting point well before noon by the traditional means of horseback as mandated by the Vatican's long history, while a sixth drove a nondescript sedan. Both Cyril and Geoffrey felt an immediate rapport with the impressive individual who had been put in charge.

Dante Fratto.

In his late thirties or early forties, he was not an especially tall man, just shy of five feet, nine inches, but well muscled with strong-looking shoulders. He had a rugged face, though not a dissipated one by any means, a face that indicated he kept himself from riotous living, with its pronounced cheekbones, strong jawline, brown eyes that sparkled with emotion and intelligence, relatively smooth skin with some scars and blemishes but no splotches, and lips that were disfigured in the center.

His voice was both commanding and down to earth.

"I was born with my upper and lower lips joined together," he explained without any self-consciousness. "At first, after they were separated, my speech was affected, and I had the most terrible pain, especially when I had to be fed. But I grew out of that, given a few years of practice and despite the ridicule of schoolmates."

"You speak well," Cyril told him, not without some admiration. "Your previous problems have all been resolved."

Fratto was obviously grateful to hear that compliment from someone of such apparent breeding.

"My education gave me some confidence," he said. "Such training reinforced my will power. Besides, the Vatican insists that everyone fill in whatever holes might exist in their education. They want to present a proper impression before the public."

Each of the guards wore a freshly laundered red and white striped outfit and Fratto was no exception. But telling their rank was impossible to an outsider.

"We should be there by evening," he said.

He rode his horse next to the sedan, at times on the driver's side, at times on the passenger's. When they stopped to rest and water the horses, Cyril and Geoffrey took the opportunity to talk with Dante Fratto.

"Are you aware that your name means 'close to a briar patch?' " asked Cyril.

"I am surprised that you know."

"It is a hobby of mine. And I have a good memory."

Geoffrey then told Fratto the meaning of his own name.

"Mine isn't very interesting," Cyril revealed. " 'Dweller near Fother's ravine' is as far as it goes."

"I come across many different kinds of names on the Internet," Fratto commented. "The only trouble is trying to unravel those that are real from those that are phony 'screen names.' "

"You do much Web-surfing?" Geoffrey asked.

"In my position, you would agree that I can't visit Rome's

bars every night!" the other man laughed good-naturedly.

"You spoke of the difficulty of trying to find out what is real on the Internet," Cyril interjected, "and what is make-believe. Have you run across anything unusual lately?"

"I have."

"Care to elaborate?"

"Weird business."

Cyril and Geoffrey quickly glanced at one another.

"How weird?"

"Lord Fothergill, think of the most obscene and satanic thoughts that anyone could have, and there is your answer."

"Any ideas as to why now?"

"I have not yet recovered from the shock to analyze the hows and whys, sir," Fratto replied without guile.

"Anything to do with young people?" Cyril asked.

"Everything, Lord Fothergill, everything to do with young people."

Geoffrey decided to gamble a bit and ask the man about Baldasarre Gervasio.

Fratto's genial manner vanished.

"Has my friend said something offensive?" Cyril probed.

Fratto's face paled somewhat and he seemed to choke momentarily.

"Forgive me, gentlemen," he apologized. "The very name chills my bones."

"Rest assured that we have heard similar opinions from others," Geoffrey stated.

"Gervasio is not a good man."

"Why, then, does the holy father put up with him instead of dismissing him immediately?" Cyril asked.

"Even Christ had His Judas."

"But remember, Christ was not fooled," Cyril reminded him. "He knew about His betrayer. But He did nothing because what was happening had been ordained."

"Is the rat man ordained then?" Fratto offered, his extraordinary candor winning over Cyril and Geoffrey.

Those not already under Gervasio's strange "spell" seemed to speak of him in precisely that manner.

"In the same sense as Judas, no, I cannot believe that he is."

Fratto paused, needing to decide how far to go with these men who were basically nothing more than strangers to him.

"There has been talk of an assassination," he said slowly.

"Against Adolfo?" Geoffrey asked, alarmed.

"No, against Baldasarre Gervasio. Respect for Pope Adolfo is plummeting but not to the point of his ouster."

"Who would be behind it?"

"I cannot say. I can only hope that they are successful."

"You have no idea then."

"Only suspicions."

"Whom do you suspect?"

"Cardinals alert to Gervasio and bravely willing to rid the Vatican of him by whatever means are available."

"Are they the only ones you have in mind?"

"Lord Fothergill, it could be the young ones especially," Fratto added. "At times, I think more them than the cardinals."

"The young ones?"

"Those no longer being fooled into believing that Gervasio is interested only in their welfare."

Scratching the back of his neck, Geoffrey decided to steer the conversation in another direction.

"I have no impression of Adolfo that leads me to think he is a simpleton, if you will pardon the expression. So how could this have happened?"

Fratto motioned for them to step farther away from the other men.

"Go ahead. . ." Cyril said a moment later.

"It is not just the presence of Gervasio, though much of this devilishness must surely stem from him. There is an evil pallor over everything, a dark feeling of defeat before the coming forces of darkness. Everywhere I turn, I—"

Suddenly Fratto's mouth dropped open and he began to stagger.

He had been felled by the red-tinged point of an arrow lodged in his back, a medieval method of death still used in a modern era apparently because it was utterly quiet. Blood began to stain the front of his uniform from his chest to his stomach and to dribble down both legs.

The five remaining men who had been sitting and resting jumped to their feet.

"*Dante!*" they yelled as one.

The road was a pass through one of the seven hills or mountains near Rome, hills which clustered all together within the city's boundaries. There were any number of ledges on that one side alone that the attacker could have used, then dashed into one of the caves to keep from being seen.

Dante Fratto was only a few seconds from death as his five comrades bent down around him.

"*They want to stop these men meeting with the holy father. . .*" he muttered. "*Do. . .not. . .let. . .that happen.*"

"We will protect them with our lives!" they cried.

He made the sign of the cross and then closed his eyes.

"*Father God. . .*" Fratto whispered, his lips parting in a smile, and then his body trembled, an instant later becoming more rigid.

CHAPTER 3

The collective reaction of the remaining Vatican guards to the sudden death of their comrade was a restrained one. They had been so well trained, indoctrinated in fact, that they managed to keep their emotions from any wild extremes that would influence their ability to think and act coherently.

Cyril spoke to one of them about their remarkable hold on themselves.

"If we were not instructed this way," the man replied, "we would endanger the lives of the rest of us. We are, in some ways, a single unit, pledged to act together for the good of that unit."

His voice broke a bit as he added, "The time when we will give in to sorrow and loss is when we are in our homes, with our families around us, but, God willing, not before then."

Cyril suggested that the back seat of the sedan was where they could rest Dante Fratto's body. The Vatican guards' next-in-command, Alberto Liberatore, nodded appreciatively but explained that it was more consistent with their traditions for the body to be strapped to the back of the man's horse, and carried back to the Vatican in that manner.

A slight man, with thin shoulders and an otherwise bony-seeming frame, a small head but the large eyes of someone much bigger, Alberto had been affected by Fratto's death as though the other man was a brother of his own blood.

"I will be your driver now," he said.

"Lord Cowlishaw and I are honored," Cyril assured him.

"We have placed you all in great danger," Geoffrey said, seemingly distressed.

"It is what we do. It is where the Lord Jesus has put us. How could we rebel against His sovereign will?"

Liberatore climbed into the driver's side of the sedan and looked back at the body of Dante Fratto strapped expertly to his horse and covered by a piece of brown canvas.

"You and I, we have been to the gates of hell together," he said softly. "And I must go on without you, dear friend. But I know you are at peace in the presence of our blessed Creator. May we one day be together as before."

He bowed his head briefly.

"The holy father is waiting," Liberatore said finally. "We must not disappoint him."

In less than two hours they would reach the Vatican.

They would experience no more arrows, but they would encounter the routine sights of beggars along the side of the road, farmers taking care of their crops, and lovers embracing. They did notice a less commonplace vignette: several buses, most of them filled with young people of various ages.

"Is there some notable event today?" Cyril asked.

"Involving children and teenagers?" Liberatore responded, since he also had noticed the phenomenon. "Not that I know of. I must admit it is odd. I wonder if Gervasio has anything to do with it?"

The three men paled at what that might entail.

"Alberto?" Cyril asked minutes later. "Do you have any idea who attacked us?"

The subject had been avoided in the initial siege of shock after the murder had occurred. But getting the answer to that question had been nagging at Cyril and Geoffrey for hours.

"It could have been one of the Communist rebels," Liberatore said.

"Communists?" Cyril questioned the other man. "You still have to worry about them?"

"More than ever. They act entirely on their own since there is no longer any guidance from Moscow. They have become yet another terrorist group. The problem in Italy is that many elected local officials—majors, chiefs of police, magistrates, and so on—and those at the national level are Communists, though they claim the facade of respectability by disavowing the roving rebel groups. But one always wonders to what extent they are secretly funding the very people they claim they don't know."

"Why so much of this?" Cyril probed respectfully. "We certainly have some degree of lawlessness in England—it's a bit of a tradition, actually, dating back to the so-called legend of Robin Hood of 600 years ago—but hardly on the scale that you indicate here."

Liberatore seemed saddened to an even greater degree than the death of Dante Fratto had made him.

"There is more and more poverty almost daily, Lord Fothergill," he replied forlornly. "Where there are people starving by the thousands, their children crying out to them for food where none can be found, there are surely those who are compelled to raise their fists in anger and frustration, and out of the most dire need."

He sighed as other images crowded his mind.

"The bishops and others, including every member of the Vatican guard, have fresh clothes and much food and drink, as well as beds and clean sheets and much more, and yet there is so much need everywhere. I think of St. Francis and I wonder about where it is heading."

"Yet you continue to serve as you do," Geoffrey pointed out.

"Because I, too, still have a family to support, sir. I can

turn my back on principle, like most men, if the survival of my loved ones is at stake."

"But at what price?"

"I ask you this: At what price would you *stop?*"

Geoffrey's expression showed his distaste.

"If it meant choosing, in any way, between God and—"

Liberatore interrupted him.

"I know, sir, what you are about to say. I know and I understand, for while I have never been blessed with your kind of education, I have had considerably more than the average person in either of our countries."

"I did not mean to be condescending."

"Nor did I intend insolence. My best friend is dead. I am not acting as I should. Forgive me."

Geoffrey reached out his hand toward Liberatore. The other man instantly clasped it in a gesture of understanding.

They had begun climbing more mountainous terrain which rose to a moderate height, then sloped down again, ending in the legendary seven hills of Rome.

A split second later. . .

"What—?" Liberatore gasped.

Flecks of blood were being carried by the continual Mediterranean breeze and splattered on the windshield of the sedan.

"Where—?" Cyril noticed, gasping as well.

From the horses.

Their eyes.

Bleeding. . .

Without warning, the five horses of the Vatican guard staggered piteously and fell, tumbling off the side of the rather narrow road on which they had been traveling, down the mountainside, throwing their startled riders and the body of Dante Fratto either ahead of them or just behind, the men screaming with uncharacteristic fear because it happened so instantly, with no warning of any sort.

"What—?" Liberatore started to say as he slammed on the sedan's brakes, and turned off the ignition.

No one was left.

"All dead!" he screamed as he saw where the bodies had landed, their necks broken.

"We should go down and check, see if any are alive," Geoffrey offered.

"We cannot. . ." Liberatore cautioned. "We have no ropes left. No one could have anticipated anything such as this."

"Could it be the water?" Geoffrey asked.

Liberatore considered that, then shook his head.

"We are yet standing," he remarked. "I suspect it was their feed. That must be it. Their grains were poisoned."

"Then someone knows about Lord Fothergill and myself," Geoffrey mused, but without saying more than that.

Yet, in Geoffrey's mind there was a very large gulf between knowing they were coming and knowing the precise nature of their mission, with Edling and Adolfo being the only others who were aware and—

Geoffrey's hands folded into tightened fists.

Baldasarre Gervasio!

"We must hurry!" Liberatore told them, "and send a properly equipped group to bring the bodies back, with the hope that—"

He collapsed into Cyril's arms.

"I am so ashamed!" he said. "Please forgive me."

Finally, the group of three reached what was left of the once majestic Forum, encountering the usual chaotic Rome traffic, and then were past it, arriving at the edge of St. Peter's Square.

"Behold!" Geoffrey said sardonically. "We stand in the center of vaulted Roman cultural exchange."

"You speak correctly," Liberatore agreed humorlessly.

He realized how cold he must have sounded.

"In recent months," he continued apologetically, "I have come to realize over and over that I serve my church in the shadow of where St. Paul met his death, and I want to give up everything about my service that once seemed precious to me."

"But you have been doing this for all of your adult life, and yet it was nearly fourteen centuries ago that Paul died," Cyril reminded the other man. "Why would it continue to give you such anguish? Should you not consider your proximity to the prison a blessing? I would, if I were as close as you."

Not wishing to show any disrespect, Liberatore chose his words with care before answering.

"Because, in some respects, the church I have been working for and believing in does a monumental disservice to the Christian legacy left behind by Paul and Peter and Matthew and all the other apostles, as well as the Lord Jesus Himself."

The two men saw that Alberto Liberatore was hurting.

"Do you not ever have an opportunity to speak with someone within the Vatican, despite the presence of Gervasio, about these feelings of yours?" Geoffrey asked with some sympathy. "Or have you been able to express your concerns to no one but Lord Fothergill and myself and perhaps the other guards?"

The dark circles under Liberatore's eyes seemed more emphasized as he took a moment or two to ponder his answer.

"Dissent is not encouraged," he said at last, "especially from a lowly guard. If it were to come from a cardinal perhaps, a monsignor, but not otherwise. The position you have within the church is everything."

The historic square was nearly deserted at a time in the evening when people were in their homes, enjoying their families. The few faithful who roamed about looked at the bedraggled group with some apprehension and a little curiosity.

Alberto Liberatore pointed to the famous balcony from which the pope would bless the crowd from time to time.

"Adolfo's personal living quarters are up there," he remarked. "And very well guarded, I might add."

"A man of God having to be protected like that?" Cyril speculated. "To be kept from harm? Think about that!"

"You must remember the plight of the original apostles, my friend," Geoffrey offered. "Many of those remarkable men became martyrs. All experienced the most severe of dangers at one time or another. Not one of them escaped being imprisoned, beaten, or spat upon."

Liberatore nodded in agreement. "It was not so bad until Gervasio arrived. Of course, none of the previous popes for hundreds of years back has seen fit to mix freely with the faithful masses."

"Unlike the apostles," Geoffrey added. "Not to do so then would have seemed snobbish, unloving, unchristian."

"Yes, I know that Peter and the other apostles did consider this contact with their converts absolutely crucial," Liberatore agreed. "But now that Gervasio has taken over, Adolfo is more isolated than any of his predecessors."

"To protect him? Is that the excuse?" Geoffrey asked.

"That is the official explanation."

"What about the truth?"

"To keep people from undermining Gervasio's influence, that is your truth. The holy father could have the beast jailed just by the snap of his fingers. But he has been blinded by the wiles of this wicked one. This individual is everything dark and mean and thoroughly vicious, though he manages to put on quite a facade when he is in the presence of the holy father and certain others whom he must never allow to see what he really is. They could quickly secure a humiliating end to his unfortunate reign."

He seemed almost physically ill.

"Kindness and charity are words Baldasarre Gervasio never speaks and impulses he never feels."

Liberatore glanced at Cyril with some admiration.

"I must confess to you now, Lord Fothergill, that I was surprised when I learned you both were coming."

"Do you know why we are here?" Geoffrey probed.

"I do not. But the caliber of men that you are makes me think something very serious is afoot. That can be the only reason why we were attacked."

Liberatore turned to Cyril who seemed uncomprehending.

"Do you know at all how highly respected you are, even well beyond the British Isles, Lord Fothergill?" he asked. "Not only in Italy but other countries also?"

"I have heard that from others. But I still am unconvinced as to the explanation."

"You make all the other lords seem rather fearsome and degenerate in comparison, according to the legend that is growing about you."

"But what can this be based upon? It all seems foolish and certainly unjustified."

"That time when you let all those poor people enter your castle, and then you found homes for that group of wandering, orphaned children. Those are acts of a remarkable man."

"You know about that?" Cyril responded, genuinely surprised that a purely "local" event in the course of a single evening had gained some prominence.

"I do, and Pope Adolfo does as well. That is principally

why he agreed to see you. And that is why Gervasio fears you so much."

Cyril jumped a bit at that.

"Fears me, you say?" he asked, incredulous. "A master of evil, as you have pictured him, fears someone he has never met?"

"Behind that cold, pale-white face, those tiny bloodshot eyes, that is what he feels, I think."

"If he shows no emotion, as you hint, how can you tell what he fears?"

"There was a quiver in his thunderous voice—his only real physical asset, by the way—whenever your name was mentioned," Liberatore recalled. "In fact, I only discovered that that was true as recently as one year ago when your father was in this country."

"A year ago? What are you saying? I was not aware that my father ever made it as far south as Rome."

"Not in connection with any visit down here but up north, near the border."

Cyril was becoming ever more confused.

"Why in the world would a despicable creature like Baldasarre Gervasio be remotely concerned about my father?" he asked. "Raymond Fothergill helped a great many people, period. Are you suggesting that Gervasio was so filled with loathing over any display of Christian charity that he—?"

"You never knew, did you?" Liberatore interrupted.

Cyril steeled himself for yet another revelation.

"Gervasio and Raymond Fothergill had some rather brief but important contact about three months before your father was to return to England."

"Contact? Of what sort?"

"Your father seemed to know that he did not have much

time to live. So, he decided to travel to northern Italy and take care of some final business arrangements. He and Gervasio happened to bump into one another through some coincidence."

"He had already started to work in the Vatican?"

"A year or so before, yes."

"What happened?"

"I think your father would have stayed on somewhat longer—it was a splendid little community at the base of the Italian Alps, very restful, with isolated little places where a man such as your father could spend time thinking and praying in perfect solitude before the Creator—but having met Gervasio, he knew that he had come up against pure evil, and he could not endure another minute in the other's presence or be anywhere near him."

"Did they talk at all?"

"Yes. . ." Liberatore replied, seeming hesitant.

"Go ahead," Cyril asked. "You need not be concerned about how I will react. I would be grateful just to find out something else about my father that I had not known before."

"Mostly about you."

"Me?"

"They spent much of their time together talking about you. I do not exaggerate, Lord Fothergill."

Cyril was beginning to wonder if Liberatore knew what he was talking about, or just gave that impression.

"How could you know any of this?" he asked. "How could you be certain that they talked about me?"

Liberatore smiled patiently.

"I was there, sir," he replied.

"With Gervasio and my father?"

"Yes, Lord Fothergill. You see, I had been assigned directly by Pope Adolfo to make sure that Gervasio was going to be safe. There was one other purpose which the holy father assumed would be kept secret between us."

Cyril was more confused than ever.

"Safe? Safe from whom?"

"The holy father was aware that Gervasio had his detractors. He wanted me present both as a bodyguard and to be attentive to what I heard."

"He trusted you that much."

"The holy father seemed always to trust Dante more. But my friend injured himself and could not make the journey."

"How long were you with Gervasio?"

"A month."

"And yet you picked up nothing at all that would have given you at least some early clue about his true nature? You hardly strike me as somebody who is apt to give up very easily."

"Not everyone would feel free to speak with me, as it turned out. The way I see it now, from the vantage point of hindsight, they either had been threatened or been aware of Gervasio's true leanings and wanted nothing to do with him or anyone interested in him. Those who did speak with me probably were little more than Gervasio's stooges but, of course, I could not have known any of this at the time."

"But how did I enter into it?" asked Cyril. "I thought my father seldom discussed any member of his family with a stranger."

"They were talking about good and evil. Gervasio said that he had met only a handful of good men over the years. Your father seemed to be one of them."

"But he was not without his sins."

"None of us is," Liberatore agreed.

"But Raymond Fothergill indulged more often than many

men dare to do, particularly those who call themselves Christians. So there were a greater number of sins to begin with. . . until the last few months."

"You know what Gervasio recognized though?"

"I have no idea."

"The soul of your father, Lord Fothergill—the struggle between the good that he knew he should be doing, and the sin that he should not but could never completely relinquish."

"Every man struggles that way. My father did until shortly before his death."

"But with Raymond Fothergill, it was more titanic in every way. I am sure that this was what fascinated someone like Gervasio."

"He must have hoped that he could get his claws into my father and have him tilt more and more toward the dark side of his nature," Cyril speculated, "and along the way, become unredeemable, yet another condemned and lost human being for the pits of hell."

Alberto Liberatore smiled with appreciation.

"That may well have been the case," he said. "But remember, despite Gervasio's fascination with your father's moral and spiritual struggle, it was you who seemed to intrigue him far more."

"My father was very colorful, I admit, and is that not part of the appeal of someone who led the life he did? Those who pursue unseemly ways tend to appear more flamboyant and more interesting than those who try very hard to keep a check on forbidden impulses."

Cyril frowned, having hit upon an overriding incongruity in what the other man had told him.

"I am puzzled," he admitted. "My father, ever the flashy one, the charming rascal, the one about whom stories will go on being whispered for years, and there is yours truly, predictably predictable, never more than dull and stodgy. Yet, you tell me, Baldasarre Gervasio apparently seized upon discussion about me like a cobra onto its victim's hand. Do you have any idea why he would react this way?"

"I do," Alberto Liberatore replied. "Evil is not attracted by its own kind, for evil sees no exciting conquest in that, and that is the essence of evil, you know, reaching out, grabbing souls here and there, always on a brutish hunt. After all, the devil has been seeing the darkest evil, as its creator, for all of human history. Rather, it is decency, integrity, morality, and abiding faith to which he is drawn or rather, to any man or woman who exhibits one or all of these."

Cyril finally asked a question that had been nagging at him since he had found out about Gervasio. "How is it that he has become so successful?"

"Baldasarre Gervasio started out as a flatterer, using beguiling words aimed at the conceit of each man. He knew that his ratlike appearance would not be an asset, but his words were, oh, how they were, and spoken by a magnificent voice that seemed so out of place coming from that body."

"Is he actually deformed? Face twisted, teeth protruding like fangs, eyes too large or small? Tell me, will you? I keep trying to picture him in my mind and fail."

"He is short, about five feet, two inches, thin shoulders, and he appears to have no neck at all, that bony face seemingly attached directly to his body. His arms are a bit long for the size of the rest of him, and he never seems to cut his fingernails as regularly as other Vatican officials. He has a rather strange mustache, jutting straight out from his nose."

"Like the whiskers of a rat?" Cyril offered.

"Exactly like that, Lord Fothergill. And his lips are narrow."

"Nothing grotesque, as you point out his features."

"It is his manner more than anything else that completes the picture. He is quick-moving, sir, furtive, his eyes seldom meeting yours for longer than a few seconds. When he walks, he seems to be scampering a bit."

"But Gervasio's voice, that is the one commanding part of his presence?"

"It is, sir, it is. His voice seems far better suited to a towering, handsome figure of a man, someone almost godlike in his appearance, perhaps even majestic, appealing to women and demanding of respect from men.

"But he has none of these attributes. There is only that voice. It startles you when you hear it coming from him, and you are disarmed, to a certain extent. While his body is wanting, his mind is not."

"You seem to have warded him off, while everyone around you has become entrapped."

"Not everyone. Remember, he has his enemies. I am not overwhelmed by facades, sir. I do not seek power. Others who do can be blinded very easily. I am not part of their group. I am a servant only. Gervasio has not regarded me seriously enough even to make the effort."

"I pray that, if he does, you do not fail to resist."

"And I pray that you never fail to resist Gervasio. He is not like any man either of you has ever known, I expect. After a while, you begin to wonder if he is a man at all or, instead, some demon wrapped in human flesh."

"And he sees me as a challenge someday?"

"I think you can be sure of that, Lord Fothergill."

"Do you think Baldasarre Gervasio will want to seduce me, figuratively speaking?"

"He will certainly try. And I think you must be prepared for his efforts to be more than figurative, Lord Fothergill."

"Where do we go now?" Geoffrey asked wearily, hoping he would be able to get some sleep before long.

"To the right there, see?" Liberatore said as he pointed in that direction. "Down that alleyway, then on to a side entrance reserved for the Vatican guard. We should not have any difficulty getting inside."

"Will we be staying there or outside the main walls?"

"We have been asked to take you to a suite of rooms that some consider far too luxurious for even the most honored visitor."

"What is special about them?"

"They are large. And there are a generous number of rare antiques placed throughout. The beds and other furniture were made by the finest craftsmen as a result of a specific papal order."

"How can that kind of expenditure be justified?" Geoffrey posed. "How many of the poor could have been fed? How many lives saved with proper medical care? Do you know what the 'official' explanation is?"

"Such display of luxury is meant to please those individuals whose favor the pope must retain—kings from other countries, queens as well, those people with the requisite power and prestige—and whose cooperation he covets," Liberatore expounded. "He claims that, in the long run, the church does actually benefit."

Cyril was experiencing a bitter taste in his mouth.

"That might be the case with the church but what about the cause of Christ?" he asked with justifiable cynicism. "But then Protestantism is not exempt from excess. We have only to remember the evangelical scandals of the last decade to realize that."

Then he changed the subject.

"How can we make sure that Adolfo will listen to what we are going to tell him about all that has happened?" he asked. "Or should we just keep to our original purpose for seeing him and forget the rest until later, if there is opportunity?"

That a well-known lord from England would have the pope's ear excited Alberto Liberatore, but he also had to keep in mind that he knew nothing of the purpose for their journey.

"I would encourage you not to divert attention from whatever it is that has brought you here in the first place. From what I have seen, I feel sure I can say that Adolfo is not a man who can necessarily focus well on more than one critical issue at a time. Perhaps he is able to do so, but not when I have been anywhere near him."

He paused, then added, "The other choice is that we could proceed to assassinate Gervasio!"

Both Cyril and Geoffrey gasped, neither expecting to hear anything like that.

"You are jesting?" Geoffrey asked uncertainly. "Surely you are?"

"I am, yes, but wistfully," Liberatore confirmed. "Lord Fothergill's reputation guarantees Adolfo's ear. That means any moves Gervasio makes will have to be prior to that meeting."

He sighed. "And then it will be up to what you say, hopefully with an eloquence and an urgency that will overcome what I suspect is the case with the holy father, that he is inclined to be negative because of Gervasio."

As he started to lead the way, Liberatore told them, "You have a hard task ahead, sir, whatever it is that you want to accomplish."

Cyril did not take that as any kind of nudge in the ribs to

find out more information, and so he said nothing.

"We go with the sanction of our powerful head of government," he replied, "and the protection of Almighty God. Surely that will be quite enough."

"It has not been 'enough' thus far," Liberatore said, referring to the death of Dante Fratto, "if we assume that Gervasio is behind what happened to that dear man."

"It could have been one of those Communist rebels you were talking about," suggested Cyril.

"Not likely, Lord Fothergill."

"How can you be so sure?"

"Rebels attack not just for the so-called pleasure of killing but to rob their victims of money and other valuables. And they would not have stopped at just one of us. They would have tried to kill everybody."

"That makes sense," Cyril admitted. "Yes, that makes sense."

"You come here from a different country, a quite different world altogether in many ways, a world that you control as much as any man is able," Liberatore said. "But today you have emerged in the sphere of someone who will not only disgust you but is capable of doing far more than that, if he wishes, and I cannot imagine him ever resisting his impulse toward evil."

Then his face assumed an ominous expression.

"For the moment, we must keep you both safe," he said, "at least until the audience tomorrow at noon. After that, getting you back to England will prove no less of a challenge. If Gervasio loses this one, he will not hesitate to seek revenge."

Cyril raised his voice as they came closer to the basilica.

"I think I see. . ." he said slowly, squinting in the moonlight. "Yes! Someone is standing on the balcony."

Looking up, Liberatore and Geoffrey noticed the figure as well, his white garb touched by silvery light.

"He is looking down at us!" Liberatore exclaimed.

And, then, abruptly, the robed figure was gone.

"The holy father!" Liberatore spoke with a wonderment that had dimmed little since his virginal days as a new Vatican guard. "That was Pope Adolfo. . .himself. He actually saw us! He may be coming down to greet us."

As Anglicans, Cyril and Geoffrey had little experience with Roman Catholicism and thus could not muster similar feelings of awe.

"You see the human side of the man," Cyril told him, "and yet you still react as you do?"

"I know that seems puzzling," Liberatore replied, "but I pray that the scales will be lifted from his eyes. This pope has the potential for greatness. Shall I instead pray for his downfall?"

A minute or two later, they had nearly reached the narrow alley when the elaborate front double doors, made of heavy, deeply carved wood, were thrown open. Striding toward the group of three was a frowning, genuinely concerned Pope Adolfo I, walking alone this time, though a full contingent of nervous men in clerical garb hovered just inside the main building, muttering among themselves. Disapproving of their concern, he turned around in midstride and gave them a single sharp look, the purpose of which they knew all too well.

"I know you have my welfare at heart," he told them, "but you act like children at times!"

Finally he reached the visitors.

"I am very glad you are here!" Adolfo exclaimed. "Where are the other guards?"

"May we tell you once we are inside?" Cyril asked

politely.

"Of course," Pope Adolfo said, one cheek twitching as he began to prepare himself for the awful news that would be given, "and let me know everything that happened. You need fear nothing now."

CHAPTER 4

Awakening from a few hours' sleep, Geoffrey informed Cyril that he wanted to go out for a walk. A pastime of his was studying architecture, and the Vatican contained some of the greatest structures in the world.

Restless as well, Cyril went on his own exploring.

It was nearly eight o'clock in the evening and he encountered little activity. A passing cardinal nodded politely, then continued on his way. A guard posted at the Sistine Chapel knew Cyril's name immediately and allowed him inside where he could view the newly restored legendary ceiling.

On the way out, he thanked the young guard, curiosity prompting him to ask the man how it was that he had known that a Cyril Fothergill was visiting.

"There are times when we show how well organized we can be, sir," he replied.

"Pope Adolfo must have known that I would be quite fascinated by the Sistine Chapel," Cyril told him.

"The holy father had nothing to do with it, sir."

In that single instant, Cyril's mood changed, becoming far darker.

"Who did?" he asked, suspecting that he knew the answer.

"Monsignor Gervasio, sir. He also told me that you are very welcome to go anywhere you want."

Cyril thanked him again and walked away.

He probably thought I would be unnerved by something as simple as that, he thought. *And that is exactly how I feel!*

He shook himself at the realization that, just moments ago,

these passageways that seemed to promise remarkable sights from antiquity now took on a more sinister atmosphere.

I'm heading back to my room, he told himself. *Geoffrey's probably returned and is waiting to share his experiences. Hate to admit it, but I think I need his company about now.*

But turning right instead of left, Cyril soon found himself lost in a section of the basilica that he had not seen earlier.

Then he heard voices.

Children's voices.

He had always loved children. Once he had told Elizabeth he wouldn't mind having a dozen of them, but she refused, saying, "For you, it might be a great deal of fun but after two, I've thrown in the towel. . .end of discussion."

Although it was an unusually brusque way for her to talk, he should have realized she would never possess Olympic strength and stamina, and having a whole stable of children would have destroyed her. Even with Clarice and Sarah, the birth process proved more painful and weakened her longer afterward than was the case with a great many other women. Though they never got beyond two, they toyed briefly with the idea of adopting others. The reason they did not do so arose as a result of their position in the aristocracy of England. By adopting one child or, especially, several, they might bring in a bloodline that was undesirable for one reason or another, corrupting a family lineage that had remained pure for centuries.

Children's voices. . .

He stopped and listened more carefully.

No joy. . .

He could detect no laughter, none of the spirited sounds that invariably occurred when children were together.

A light.

Ahead, light spilled out from one of the myriad of rooms

that lined every hallway he had seen thus far, some large enough to hold scores of people, others much smaller, few of them marked.

The one door just a few feet in front of him was ajar and as he reached it, he quietly stepped inside.

Dozens of children. . .

From the age of about five years on into their teens, he saw more than thirty, each seated in front of a computer monitor and a keyboard.

At first he was charmed by this, especially since it was likely that they could have been home wasting time with "junk food for the masses" on television, roughhousing with friends, or at a neighborhood movie theater watching the latest product spewed out by an increasingly vulgar industry.

So intent, he thought. *They seem oblivious to everything else.*

Most were.

Lined up in six rows of six children each, they were surfing the Internet, participating in juvenile chat rooms, and playing computer games.

One enjoying the latter caught Cyril's attention.

He put his hand on the shoulder of the redheaded, freckle-faced boy, careful not to startle him.

"It looks interesting," he remarked. "Can you tell me anything about it?"

"Would you like to play, mister?"

"I'd be happy to try. What are the rules?"

After these were explained to him in an astonishingly articulate manner, the boy, who seemed no more than twelve years old, stood and let Cyril sit down in his place. Cyril wrapped his fingers around the joystick and started right into the action.

At first it seemed no less innocent than an old-fashioned

pinball machine. but later, as each new level of play was accessed, the action became violent and, eventually, bloody. At the point Cyril stopped playing, there was an electronic representation of a man's head being blown to pieces.

"What—?" he started to say as he stood and faced the boy. "I am startled that this is allowed."

"They don't know," the boy told him.

"How many others here have access to this garbage?"

"Everyone. It's the Internet, you know, no strings attached."

Cyril knew that he could do nothing for the moment, so he walked away, perspiration starting to soak his clothes.

None of the other youngsters was playing that kind of game. Instead most were being challenged by electronic chess or math questions or doing research online presumably for some school project.

He stopped at another table where a long-haired little girl was sitting.

On the monitor screen he read the words: "*Your Part in the—*"

As soon as she saw him looking at the monitor, she turned it off, leaving the computer running.

"What are you learning?" he asked pleasantly. "Taking a part in—?"

She looked up at him, no emotion on her face.

"Let me see, please," he said as he bent over and reached for the monitor switch.

She bit him on the arm.

"*Hey!*" he yelped as he withdrew it.

The other children in that row were now standing and staring at him.

"What's going on here?" he asked with some authority.

And then he noticed something else.

The girl who had turned off the monitor had a bruise on one cheek and a cut on her earlobe. Her eyes were bloodshot.

One by one, he glanced at the others. In that same row was a little boy with a black eye. Another had an ugly scar across his temple. A little girl's left arm was in a cast.

He walked up and down the other rows and found similar sights: a boy with a patch over one eye; a teenaged girl with recent stitches from the bridge of her nose to the tip; another who had been blinded in one eye.

"What happened to you?" he asked of the group.

At first no one answered, then one of the little boys, a scar reaching from one end of his forehead to the other, handed him a four- by five-inch photo showing him with his parents.

"Did they do this to you?" he asked the child, looking at the others as well.

Most nodded.

He noticed their clothes, dirty and threadbare. Several boys wore mismatched, odd-colored socks.

"But who arranged to have you all brought here?" Cyril asked.

No response.

"And why are you here so late at night?" he pressed. "Shouldn't you be in your beds by now?"

One of the older boys, in his early teens, stepped forward. As he opened his mouth to speak, Cyril saw that most of his teeth were gone.

"Mister, we *can't* sleep," he replied. "Simple as that."

Another nodded, looking down at the bare wooden floor. "Dreams, sir. . .things our folks done to us. We can't forget. We will *never* forget."

Cyril found an empty chair and sat down.

The older boy added, "Doctor says I'm ruined, you know."

"Ruined? What do you mean?"

"Never be a father. . .never have kids of my own. My old father got mad, real mad at me a few months ago when I wouldn't sleep with him again, and he took my—"

He blushed and didn't finish.

"What's your name?" Cyril asked.

"Daniel."

"Where are you living now?"

"Someplace near here. I can't tell you where, but it's real close, mister."

"A foster home?"

"I think so."

"How long ago were you taken from your home by the authorities?"

"A few months."

Someone was tugging at Cyril's sleeve, and he recoiled when he saw who it was.

A round-faced, large-eared boy of about seven looked up at him with an expression of great sadness.

"Oh Lord!" he gasped as an instinctive prayer.

No legs, not even any stumps, and one of his arms was missing up to the elbow.

"That's Franco," the teenager named Daniel told him. "Somebody threw him on the steps."

"*Threw* him?" Cyril asked.

"I was looking out my window and I saw it, sir. They tossed him from a car window like he was a rotten melon."

Cyril reached down and picked up little Franco, wrapped his arms around that pitiable shape, and hugged him as tenderly as he could.

"And so you come here to this room and use these computers how often?" he asked Daniel.

"Three times a week."

"Are you the only ones?"

"No, sir."

"Are you sure?"

"Yes, sir. Monsignor Gervasio says that there are so many kids like us and—"

Cyril's mind seemed to spin off into another universe, and he could not hear, for however many seconds, the rest of what Daniel was saying.

Monsignor Gervasio says. . .

His hands slippery with perspiration, Cyril nearly dropped the little form in his arms but stopped just short of doing that.

Suddenly he felt something touch his right cheek.

Franco—with no legs and a much smaller body than other seven-year-olds—had reached up and kissed him.

Cyril wanted to hold himself together, but he failed and started sobbing.

"Mister, don't cry," Daniel told him. "We're alive, aren't we? That's something, isn't it? We're part of the same family now, brothers and sisters together."

Another boy, younger than he, spoke up. "The monsignor's helping us, sir. He's giving everyone a reason to go on living. All we have to do is listen to him. He'll do right by us. When we are real lonely, he lets us stay overnight with him. He doesn't force himself on us like our parents did."

Cyril's nerve ends were rebelling, pummeled by the shock of what he was hearing, the room becoming unsteady in his vision.

"I must leave now," he said.

As he started to put Franco on the floor, that little one whimpered, talking incoherently, trying to pull himself with his only full arm back onto the stranger's lap, something he had avoided for a very long time with other men he had met. This man seemed different, kinder, and wouldn't it be wonderful if he stayed longer?

"No. . .no. . ." Cyril said. "Please, I must—"

Daniel stalked over and grabbed Franco, a flash of anger twisting his young face.

"Go then, mister!" he declared.

"But I—"

"You have your world, we have ours. Only the monsignor really understands."

A girl perhaps Daniel's age added, "Only the monsignor is giving us a chance to—"

Daniel shot her a sharp glance and she cut herself off.

Less than a minute later, every child in that room was back at a computer, at times typing feverishly. Even Franco was placed in a chair quite different from the others, with padding on the seat to ease the pressure on his legless lower body.

. . .*you have your world, we have ours.*

Cyril shut the door behind him and stood in the corridor, his eyes closed briefly. Then he headed back the way he had come, toward the main entrance of St. Peter's.

More than anything else now, he needed some fresh air.

Yet, suddenly, there was Geoffrey Cowlishaw, his voice sure and strong. "Glad I found you. Adolfo would like to see us now, in addition to tomorrow. Let's go!"

Chapter 5

Pope Adolfo was deeply grieved by the loss of so many of his Vatican guards. But he was a man who had learned to subjugate his feelings as much as possible since he was on display a large part of the time and found it unwise to let everyone see him wearing emotions on his sleeve. . .

"Yes, I know, our time is set for tomorrow, but I thought this would be pleasant, and nourishing," Pope Adolfo remarked to Cyril and Geoffrey. The three men were seated in the private papal dining room at a simple square table with equally plain high-backed chairs, hardly part of the extravagant image that had been painted for the guests. The two papal visitors had just finished an impromptu and relatively simple dinner of Lombard chicken pasties, golden leeks and onions, and green pea pottage. "But now that Dante Fratto has been murdered, I can only believe that your mission here is even more urgent, if that is possible, than your prime minister mentioned."

"Do you know anything about why we were sent, sir?" Cyril asked, not wanting to contradict whatever it was that Edling might have mentioned.

"I was told it was a life-or-death matter," the pontiff replied. "And I have come to know that Edling is not one to use words lightly. Despite the clear theological differences that have hobbled the relationship between us, I trust that he and I can claim more than a modicum of respect for one another."

"Edling did not exaggerate, sir," Cyril assured him. "But there is now much more involved than when we left

England."

"Go ahead," Adolfo urged. "You can be as frank as you may wish this night, in this very private room. Only the three of us and the Holy Spirit are here now. Nothing goes beyond these walls unless we all agree that it should."

Cyril was aware of the hour and he did not want to risk tiring out their host, who was known to become rather nasty if he stayed up past a certain hour.

"It is very late. . ." he began. "Would you not prefer to wait until tomorrow?"

"I can do that, of course, I can, for I make my own rules naturally, but you would satisfy me if you told me but a little so that I may sleep on it."

"Islamic terrorists. . ."

"Are their kind stirring up trouble again?"

"They have devised a way of devastating Europe without a single legion being sent out on a single battlefield," Cyril told him.

Adolfo found that appalling but he was also skeptical.

"The very thought is bloodcurdling," he said, "but my rational mind cannot conceive how this would be possible. I do not mean to question your veracity or good sense, but you must admit that what you have just said seems preposterous."

Cyril swallowed hard a couple of times.

"Plague. . ."

"Plague?" the pontiff repeated. "Surely you are not advancing this in any serious way. And yet. . . you are hardly a man to be facetious under the present circumstances."

"We have reason to believe that a plan has been developed to make the continent a wasteland of pestilence, with tens of millions of people dead, entire villages, towns, and cities wiped out. Rome itself would become a graveyard!"

Abruptly, Adolfo's right hand started shaking noticeably

and he quickly clamped his left one over it.

"What a ghastly thought that is!" he exclaimed. "I am giving my very life to this city. I love every ancient corner of it. I—"

He cut himself off.

"Continue, gentlemen," he half-whispered.

"We need to do something decisive before the enemy commences," Cyril said. "If plague were unleashed, we would find ourselves fighting on two fronts. We could win against a flesh-and-blood enemy but lose the other war!"

Adolfo's eyes widened, and he started breathing a bit more rapidly.

"My voice calling Christendom to a unified front, is that it?" he asked. "Forget our divisions? Bury our grievances? Unite for the sake of our common survival against the newest barbarian hordes?"

"Precisely," Geoffrey added, knowing that appealing to the man in this way was calculating, but he was willing to use almost any tactic if necessary. "Should you and Edling and others be able to reach an agreement, I have no doubt that we can put together an army of dedicated soldiers who would march to the very center of Islam and defeat the enemy. This time they would be truly vanquished, with little chance of posing a threat again."

Cyril thought of Roger Prindiville, aging but still able, someone who would be reborn if he could participate in new battles for the survival of western civilization.

"We have learned from the mistakes of Richard the Lion-hearted, as well as some of the Vatican's own great men," he pointed out, "and we have learned to avoid the excesses of those who followed in Richard's footsteps."

Cyril realized that some of the Vatican's greatest treasures had been nothing but booty from the earlier Crusades, possessions basically stolen from conquered foes, so he avoided going into further detail.

"I have listened, as you can tell," Adolfo told them as he held out his hand. "And I have no doubt of your sincerity. But I shall have to take this up with my advisors, particularly the one who is chief over them all. In fact, he has been scolding me lately for my own harsh views on Islam, and he wants me to meet with some of their leaders as a gesture of tolerance. After all, he is the man who persuaded me that the Vatican should have a Web site so that we can easily communicate with people everywhere, and they with us."

Immediately Cyril and Geoffrey knew of whom he was speaking. More importantly, they had their first official glimpse of Baldasarre Gervasio's influence.

"I am dubious, yes," Adolfo concluded, "but I must bring him into this matter before making a decision."

Cyril and Geoffrey held back any reaction to that statement, letting Adolfo continue without interruption.

"How did you come across this information?" he asked. "That would be a key, of course. Your sources need to be investigated."

"We cannot do that," Cyril said.

"And what stops you?"

"We do not know where and who they are."

Adolfo leaned back and slapped his knees.

"I am astonished, gentlemen!" he exclaimed. "You think the world as we know it could come to an end very soon, I gather, and you base that upon what?"

"A man I respect who overheard two apparent terrorists conversing," replied Cyril.

Adolfo was adjusting his robes as he stood.

"After breakfast," he said, "the three of us will meet for as long as you wish."

Neither of them misunderstood what he was trying as discreetly as possible to tell them, that their time was at an end, and he wanted to hear nothing further until the morning.

"There is something else," Cyril remarked, his palms cold and clammy.

"What is this?" the pope asked irritably. "Did I not tell you that we could take up where we have left off—"

"It's about the circumstances of your half brother's death," Cyril interrupted. "I thought you would want to know. We both were there."

The pope seemed to stagger.

"My brother is *dead?*" Adolfo asked incredulously.

"You did not know?"

"He kept our relationship hidden from almost everyone. That you know of it is a confidence he rarely granted."

He leaned against the whitewashed wall.

"I must sit down again," he told them.

They helped him to the chair.

"That poor soul. . ." he moaned. "Tell me, please, what happened. Leave out nothing, I beg you, gentlemen."

Adolfo was a man who seemed always in control of himself, camouflaging his real emotions. But for the first time since they had arrived, both men witnessed a crack in the papal armor.

"Was there much pain?" he asked after Cyril had related Captain Letchworth's final moments.

"That is doubtful, sir," Geoffrey replied.

"Dumb beasts showing such kindness. . ." Adolfo said. "I think my brother could inspire that in everyone—"

Tears seeped out of the corners of his eyes.

"—but me," he finished. "One of my life's deepest regrets," he muttered. "I paid little of the attention to him that I should have. I was so heavenly minded that I became no earthly good in his regard. He was, in the days when we were toget-her, interested only in pursuits that took him outdoors. My brother disliked the four walls of any building, no matter how majestic."

"He mentioned you more than once," Cyril recalled. "I detected no animosity, sir, only a desire for the wall between the two of you to be brought down."

"You have done something special for me," he told them. "I pray that I shall not disappoint you."

As Pope Adolfo opened the door, a short man who had been waiting patiently in the hallway outside brightened up.

"You had asked me to remind you about Monsignor Gervasio," he said. "Do you want to see him in a few minutes?"

"It is too late. Early in the morning, before I meet with our special visitors again. I have to spend time on something else tonight and cannot allow myself to be distracted."

He pointed toward Cyril and Geoffrey.

"Please escort my guests to their rooms," he said, "and kindly make sure that they have whatever they need."

"Your Holiness?" the man asked.

Adolfo told him to go ahead and speak.

"There is one matter I should mention to you, if you will give me leave."

Cyril felt some sympathy for this frail-looking little man, in large measure because of his appearance. Little more than a large midget in size, he didn't seem to possess the stamina to last much longer at whatever his duties happened to be.

Noticing his transparent expression, Adolfo said, "Good Thomas here has never been a robust sort of man. I thank our gracious Lord Jesus for keeping him as well as he is for the time that he has been able to serve the church. Each day my dear brother in Christ has is truly a blessing for the rest of us.

"Sometimes, to my shame, I lose my temper with him. . . but I always apologize before the day is over so that the sun does not go down on my wrath, which often is little justified, certainly if Thomas is the object.

"I often think that my thorn in the flesh is a willingness to be too hard on those who have little opportunity to fight back. There are others I could criticize much of the day every day but this dear soul is not one of them."

Both Cyril and Geoffrey were impressed by Adolfo's openness and could not imagine Edling displaying similar candor in front of strangers.

"You are not accustomed to a powerful man airing his shortcomings like that, are you?" he asked.

They shook their heads.

"It is one of the strengths that we display here," Adolfo remarked, "one of the many, I should add."

He leaned forward and kissed the other man once on each pale, wrinkled cheek.

"Now what is it that you wanted to tell me, good Thomas?" he asked warmly.

"Monsignor Gervasio sends his regrets that he will not be able to join you for dinner tomorrow evening. He must entertain several special young people who have flown here from the United States."

Thomas smiled weakly before continuing.

"Monsignor Gervasio wanted to let you know now rather than in the morning in the event that you would be able to make other plans. After all, he acknowledges how busy you have become of late. Your overture to those—"

Thomas's gaze darted to the two visitors and he stopped himself.

Adolfo was distressed, but not at the other man.

"I have seen far less of the monsignor than usual during the past several weeks. Why is that, can you tell me? It would not be to his advantage to appear as though he is deliberately avoiding me."

Cyril noticed the implied threat coming from a man of God, a threat that seemed based more upon personal offense than any moral or spiritual issue.

At that point Thomas appeared quite uncomfortable.

"I am sure that he intends no disrespect," he hastened to add.

But Adolfo was exasperated.

"You are not also going to tell me what I so strongly suspect, are you?" he asked. "Surely you are not."

Thomas could not meet his steady gaze.

"I am afraid your suspicions are correct. He is having some difficulty with those new 'pets' of his, sir."

The pope shook his head in amazement.

"The affairs of the world take second place?" he demanded.

"I think it is simply that he feels he can do whatever he wants on his own time, time you have given him for rest and relaxation."

"You speak well, but then what difficulty could he be having that demands so much of that free time you have so eloquently defended?" Adolfo asked disbelievingly, his hands on his hips. "How can Christ's vicar be competing for time against them?"

Thomas's face was whiter than usual.

"They have been reproducing considerably faster than he originally anticipated," he explained carefully. "Sadly, Monsignor Gervasio thinks that he may soon have to destroy quite a few, or let a large number loose."

. . .or let a large number loose.

As Adolfo shivered visibly at the prospect, Cyril and Geoffrey could only wonder what was going on.

"I thought it was a foolish hobby to begin with," the pope said, "but then, I must say, he certainly has the right to be foolish, if that is what he wishes."

He sighed expansively. "I do hope, though, that my dear Baldasarre turns his attention to cats or ferrets eventually or perhaps parrots, yes, parrots can be interesting. Any of those creatures is so much more pleasant."

Adolfo then turned to face Cyril and Geoffrey.

"My special assistant is certainly not without his share of quirks," he explained almost defensively. "For one thing, gentlemen, it seems that he enjoys the company of rats. Is that not bizarre for someone of such seeming intelligence to find delight in those scampering things of dark alleys and dank catacombs? Monsignor Baldasarre Gervasio claims he can train the creatures to do anything he wants."

CHAPTER 6

*. . .those scampering things of dark alleys and dank cata-
combs? Monsignor Baldasarre Gervasio claims he can train
the creatures to do anything he wants.*

Cyril had no doubt that Adolfo's observation was on
Geoffrey's mind as well, for it could hardly be otherwise to
someone as perceptive and intelligent.

*. . .he is the man who persuaded me that the Vatican
should have a Web site so that we can easily communicate
with people everywhere, and they with us.*

Neither Cyril nor Geoffrey was about to broach the subject because its implications chilled their blood, and they
dreaded being drawn into it, and becoming distracted from
concentrating on probably the most important meeting they
would ever have.

*Someone who was himself described by his detractors as
ratlike in appearance was now engaged in breeding them,*
Cyril thought. *Adolfo seems to be indebted to Gervasio in
some way.*

He could feel his chest tightening as he contemplated
that.

And Baldasarre Gervasio had become so successful in his
"hobby" that he might have to release many rats or kill
them, or perhaps both.

No one within the Vatican had seen any reason to stop
Baldasarre Gervasio, at the beginning or later. He had been
allowed to pursue his unabashedly bizarre hobby, one quite
out of character for someone of his position within the church,

as long as he continued to serve the church and its papal authority well in all other respects.

I want to call them little more than fools, he thought, *but if they are not aware of any danger, then why would they act?*

Cyril finally drifted into sleep but not before he imagined bloodred eyes staring at him from the darkness of his room, and the sound of scampering little feet moving closer to his bed.

Cyril was not surprised when he was able to sleep only for an hour but then awoke covered in perspiration, though the temperature was chilly. He switched from trying to sleep on his right side to his left and willed his eyes to stay closed but nothing worked, nothing permitted him to stay asleep for more than some miserable fits and starts, and so he remained on his back, unmoving, looking up at the white ceiling. Geoffrey, he imagined, was spending the night in much the same turmoil.

But after getting up and putting on some heavier clothes, he stood before his friend's door and heard nothing.

You might be better off than I am after all, he thought, smiling. *You could hardly be sleeping less than I did. I am not normally afraid of rats, but this time—!*

Cyril walked down one hallway, then another, down a flight of stairs, and into a large foyer, until he finally approached the guard at the main entrance.

"Is it safe out there at an hour past midnight?" he asked.

"Right here, sir, yes, it is," the tall, handsome young man with a square jaw and slightly pockmarked cheeks answered. "Two or three blocks away, in either direction, well, I would have to give you another answer."

"I will not stray beyond the piazza," Cyril assured him.

The guard started to open the large double doors.

"You are a Vatican guard, are you not?" Cyril asked, knowing the answer to such an obvious question.

"I am, sir."

"My name is Cyril Fothergill. What is yours, young man?"

"Eduardo Pintozzi, sir. Pleased to meet you."

"Do you know where Alberto Liberatore is right now? And what is going to be done with Dante Fratto's body?"

The guard froze with the doors halfway open. Alarmed, Cyril asked, "Is there something wrong?"

"Forgive me, sir. Dante Fratto was my closest friend."

"I should have been more sensitive."

"You could not have known."

"But I might have suspected it," Cyril added. "I gather the guards are a very close-knit group."

"We all do our best in this life, sir."

"Some do, I suppose. The rest, who can be sure?"

"I was sure about Dante."

They both were outside now, standing at the edge of the piazza.

"How bad has it been?" Cyril inquired.

The other man stiffened, saying nothing.

"You are under no obligation to answer that," Cyril assured him. "If I have gone too far, just say so."

Pintozzi nodded as he said, "I know, sir. It is very difficult for me, for the rest of us. It was difficult for poor Dante."

"Because of Gervasio?"

The young man glanced from side to side.

"No other reason," he said.

"Is this pope of yours really so ignorant that he simply cannot see the truth or, seeing it, does not have the courage to break away from a man who could end up dismantling the church as we know it?"

Cyril spoke with deliberate harshness because he wanted to

provoke an impassioned response, not a carefully rehearsed one.

"The holy father is not stupid!" Pintozzi replied, irritated at what an outsider was saying. "You shall not judge, sir!"

Cyril softened his voice.

"But, remember, young man, Scripture also indicates that by their fruits ye shall know them. Adolfo's fruits at this point appear like rotten apples. How could I think otherwise when he seems to be ignoring so much?"

"If you are in a room, sir, and there is only one door, and your sole contact with the outside world is what passes through the doorway, are you ignorant because you trust the man in charge of it to give you the truth, whatever the consequences?

"In the beginning, this individual seems to prove himself very well indeed, and so you begin to trust him more and more. Day by day, you depend on him to an ever greater extent, in major ways as well as minor ones.

"After a while, you tell yourself that there can never be a reason to distrust him, and so whatever he says, you go along. Not to do so would be a betrayal of all that he seems to have done for you, all that he seems to have done for the church."

He then turned to face Cyril.

"May I speak freely?"

"You may."

"How long have you known Lord Cowlishaw?"

"Less than a month."

"Do you trust him, sir?"

"Completely."

"The holy father has known Monsignor Gervasio for more than two years. Should he trust the man any less?"

Cyril hated the comparison but he saw Pintozzi's point.

"Touché!" he replied, admiring the younger man's intellectual agility. "Can anything be done?"

Pintozzi pondered that briefly as Cyril and he stood in the center of the piazza.

"Liberatore and I or any of the other guards could be imprisoned and executed for heresy if we attempted to talk to the holy father."

"Just for talking to the man?"

"That is what Monsignor Gervasio claims."

"And you could do nothing to protect yourselves?"

"We do not have the same rights as the cardinals and others. Anything that happens to them is a matter of immediate concern. For my comrades and myself, it would be swept under the rug and forgotten."

Eduardo Pintozzi half-smiled as he added, "It is a miracle that Gervasio has allowed you any sort of contact with the holy father."

"Prime Minister Edling of England has asked for this audience. Even Gervasio cannot easily stifle a request from someone such as that."

"I suggest that your influential prime minister needs to tell him more. I suggest also that the president of France and the rulers of other countries must band together. If they agreed on a message, they would be heard by the holy father."

Pintozzi looked at Cyril briefly, as though pondering what he would say next, then asked a question that could not have been anticipated.

"Do you know. . ." he spoke nervously, ". . .about Monsignor Gervasio's experiments?"

Cyril felt an odd kind of paralysis grip his throat. He wanted to swallow but could not. He wanted to breathe but he was unable. And as a result he became dizzy.

Pintozzi kept him from falling.

"You should go back inside, Lord Fothergill," he urged.

"The air. . ." Cyril muttered. "I need the air."

He forced himself to inhale, exhale, inhale, exhale, again and again.

Feeling returned.

He could swallow though his throat was laced with throbbing pain, and a headache hit him, the worst he had had for decades.

Do you know about Monsignor Gervasio's experiments?

"Experiments?" he asked. "There have been experiments? What do you know about these?"

"Not a great deal," Pintozzi assured him. "And I may be exaggerating without intending to, but I have seen something that, along with comments overheard, makes me question, makes me want to know a great deal more."

"What did you see?"

"Monsignor Gervasio ordered Dante Fratto and me to find a poor man from the streets, preferably one quite emaciated and otherwise looking poorly, anyone fitting that description, and promptly bring him back to the basilica."

"For what earthly reason?" Cyril was dreading where this exchange would lead.

"He said he wanted to help the poor soul. He had some new medicine, medicine that might help him put some weight back on."

"And you had no choice but to obey."

"We had no reason to question the order in the first place. It seemed born of a charitable gesture on his part."

Cyril's stomach was tightening.

"What became of this man?"

"That. . .that is where this whole ungodly nightmare became the most discomforting, Lord Fothergill."

Pintozzi thought he heard a sound behind him and turned

sharply but saw nothing and relaxed a bit.

"I saw the man three days later," he said.

"Where?"

"Give me a moment, sir, if you will. It was so horrible."

Cyril respected that request.

Finally, Pintozzi, looking less like a courageous Vatican guard and more like a man who had witnessed the nightmare of his life, spoke again, his voice trembling.

"He must have escaped somehow," he said.

"Escaped from what?"

"I have no idea, Lord Fothergill. I just know his appearance."

Pintozzi became ill then, in the center of the piazza known as St. Peter's Square. Standing by his side, Cyril quickly handed him a silk handkerchief so that the young man could wipe his mouth and chin. Amusingly to Cyril, he was careful to keep his uniform clean, a reflexive act trained into him over the course of the few years he had spent in service to the papacy.

"There were sores all over his flesh, sir," Pintozzi managed to say after his stomach had calmed down. "They were filled with greenish liquid—"

Again his stomach reacted to the images in his mind.

Eduardo Pintozzi was very weak after this latest attack had passed, and he plopped down on the hard stone of St. Peter's Square.

"I am so sorry, Lord Fothergill," he moaned. "I could not control myself. That poor, poor man looked much worse than I have described. I have not told you everything because I wanted to spare you some of the details.

"Something was, I think, literally eating at that man from inside his body. He fell not more than ten feet from me, hitting the ground like an overripe melon. A cry of pain issued from his mouth, and then. . .then he was gone."

Pintozzi's blue eyes were wide as he looked at Cyril.

"Something happened to him behind those walls," he said, pointing back at the basilica. "Something that must have been so awful—"

"I know what it was," Cyril told him.

"How could you, Lord Fothergill? I mean no disrespect, but you did arrive here a mere few hours ago."

"I can tell you that what you have described is an important part of that which brought me here."

"Praise God!" Pintozzi exclaimed. "I think the whole church is going to explode, like that poor man's ugly, festering boils, if something is not done: It is not just Monsignor Gervasio, though he is the most serious threat, sir. He is here today because he has been allowed to be here."

"Gervasio as a product of the state of Catholicism. . ." Cyril mused. "Interesting notion, young man, very interesting."

"Lord Fothergill," Pintozzi continued, "I am a Catholic. I have been all my life, and I expect always to be a Catholic."

Cyril found himself admiring this young man.

"The church has had a long history, one filled with martyrs whom we admire to this day. But I think the Catholic Church will not survive until the Second Coming if something is not done to correct the abuses.

"Remember, I am not a Catholic. Nor is my friend, Lord Cowlishaw. We are what we are because of doctrinal disagreements that have attached themselves to the church."

Cyril was gaining respect for what training and education the Vatican had invested in its guards, with this man as a superior example.

"But, then, it goes deeper," Pintozzi was telling him. "Baldasarre Gervasio is a symptom in addition to whatever else he might be, and I think when you say that the whole

Roman Catholic Church is going to—"

He stopped. Both men froze. A few feet away was a large rat.

"Speak of the devil," Cyril muttered.

It seemed merely to be looking at them.

"Behind you!" Pintozzi exclaimed.

A dozen rats had gathered on the piazza.

. . . on the ground, not moving, just studying the two of them.

More were coming from the basilica, from around the sides of the cross-shaped building built during the reign of Constantine, the dark narrow alleys suffused with the odor of age. . .a score of rats, a hundred, one after the other, then that first wave stopped.

Cyril and Eduardo Pintozzi stood without moving.

"Should we not run before more come after us?" the younger man asked.

"Why are they coming from the basilica?" Cyril asked. "You have neighborhoods on all sides of this property, especially those quite a bit nearer water, that are far more likely to spawn such numbers."

"We used to scour the place for them," Pintozzi remarked.

Cyril knew what the other man was going to say next, not out of any ability to read his mind, but, more than likely, the leading of the Holy Spirit.

"He claimed he wanted to clean them up," Pintozzi went on, "and, among other things, raise them as pets for children, not as creatures to be feared. Any symbol of evil that is regenerated can be a triumph for the church, he claimed. If people did not shun them, the rats would not be forced to live in places and in ways that fostered disease."

"Pets for children?" Cyril repeated, chills racing along his spine. "Has that started as yet?"

"Not for another few months or later. But the monsignor is not stopping there, from what I understand. He wants every family in Rome to have one, compliments of the church. And he will encourage every family to raise them as well, shipping them to friends and relatives throughout Europe."

"With such grand plans, why wait? Why delay?"

"He is not satisfied that they are sufficiently docile. He wants more than one generation to become used to captivity."

Both men were silent again as more rats came into view, several hundred now in the piazza.

"We should go now," Cyril urged, "but slowly. I hope they react as other predators. Something that is fast moving becomes a target, something that moves slowly a mere curiosity."

The double doors at the front of St. Peter's, usually opened to receive the faithful from many countries. . .

That was where they would head. They could not make it across the huge square before being overrun.

Only the basilica offered sanctuary.

And so they walked, an inch at a time. Neither could move faster and risk stirring up the hordes of rats now momentarily placid. But there was also another reason, an unnerving one.

The hundred rats or so of minutes earlier had become a thousand, a thousand had expanded to a few thousand, and the influx was not ceasing at that.

The rats seemed to be communicating with one another at the same time, strange little sounds, each tiny mouth moving, issuing whatever its "call" was and joining the others in a growing, nerve-tingling chorus. Such a combination of sounds had made Cyril and Pintozzi sweat, and their clothes were now drenched and sticking to every inch of their flesh as though the fabric had become part of the living skin.

"Is this a hint of hell?" the younger man whispered. "Are

these not rats at all but demons disguised?"

"With Gervasio involved," the older statesman advised, "you may not be far from the truth."

Every step they took now meant wading through the gray-coated creatures, their rodent musk odor strong. Many skittered to one side. But the rest reared up on their hind legs, snouts moving as they took in the smell of human beings.

"My leg!" Pintozzi exclaimed. "They are climbing up—"

"Steel yourself," Cyril begged him. "You must not allow panic to control you. They will sense your fear, they will smell it, and that will drive them mad."

"One of them is on my—"

His shoulder.

The rat was positioned there, examining his face, concentrating on the tender eyes, the moist, tender eyes. But only for a brief moment. And then it lunged forward, biting into—

Pintozzi screamed in agony. And then he started to run. As he reached the heavy double doors, he closed his fingers around the handle and pulled on it, expecting the massive entry to swing open and he could rush inside, slamming it shut behind him.

But the doors were stuck. . .or barred from the other side!

Pintozzi recoiled abruptly in the most intense fear of his young life, and then he began beating his fists on the engraved wood so hard, ignoring some sharp edges, that his hands started bleeding. Not just thin trickles but gushing spurts of it, seemingly unstoppable, trickling down his arm, and then onto his chest and legs.

In an instant, it seemed, a horde of rats was covering his entire body, muffling his screams, dropping him to the ground as their sharp teeth tore at him, reducing his uniform to shreds as they went for his flesh.

Cyril could have stayed where he was, could have valiantly

tried to rescue the other man, but there were by then thousands of seemingly ravenous creatures in the piazza, perhaps as many as ten thousand or more.

No chance.

He would not have a chance if he remained there.

For the moment, the rats seemed to have forgotten him, and that gave Cyril a chance to seek refuge he felt only St. Peter's could give, not back across the square and into the city.

The alley. The one that another Vatican guard, Alberto Liberatore, had indicated to Geoffrey and him only a few hours before. Cyril ran toward it, slipping once, hitting the ground hard, then scrambling back to his feet, and heading into the alley.

It was narrow and had the scent of a graveyard.

He tried the first door.

Unmovable.

The next could not be opened either. Door after door, blocked from the other side, as solid an obstruction as a stone wall.

Cyril stood now near the end of the alley. Behind the basilica was a pleasant little courtyard, with several varieties of trees, some rosebushes, and benches to sit on for a moment of quiet contemplation.

He glanced behind him. Miraculously, none of the rats had followed him.

While Cyril had escaped, at least momentarily, he had no doubt that Gervasio, the one responsible for what had just happened, would not let him alone. His body was trembling as he thought, suddenly, of Dante Fratto.

"If there can ever be a humane murder," he whispered, "it was yours. It is a tragedy that you died, yes, but a blessing that your death was as quick as it was, and that your attacker did not want you to linger for his pleasure."

Not like Eduardo Pintozzi. . .

Thousands of rats tearing at his flesh.

By now the creatures, as emblematic of evil as snakes and bats, would surely have finished their grisly feast. The horde would be returning to their nests or, emboldened by the smell and the taste of already shed blood, setting out to hunt him down.

That image seemed to wrap around every cell of Cyril's brain, every nerve in his taut body, tempting him to act with consuming irrationality, tempting him to run, forget common sense, and run as far away from the threat as he could. But such an escape would draw them to him as readily as blood and the odor of sweat and fear, for rats could lock onto it in the night as unerringly as sharks drawn to their prey.

His gaze roamed the courtyard.

Open. Far too open. Not even a few trees offered sanctuary.

The rats could climb any one in seconds.

Cyril noticed a door that was edged by ivylike vines, an ancient door, by the look of its faded, splintering wood on rusty hinges. It offered the seedy appearance of having been utterly forgotten, without benefit of any obvious effort expended to polish or paint or otherwise renovate it as the years passed, contrary to the persistent tinkering with the rest of the basilica.

There had been a rumor that some pope someday might decide to demolish most or all of the present structure and start over but that seemed extreme, and it paid no heed to whatever archaeological treasures would be buried in the process.

Cyril pushed on the old door. Nothing happened.

A second time.

Creaking. . .

The hinges protested.

Cyril put all of his weight behind the third attempt. The door fell away, causing a thick cloud of dust and whatever else to erupt from inside the basilica, hitting the air in a suffocating blast. He did not back away in time. And it caught Cyril, doubling him over painfully as his nose and mouth were hit full force, pushing him backward as though it was something of real form and substance, and he had collided with it. He nearly blacked out. That moment felt like the approach of death itself, dust and odors from generations ago overwhelming him. After several minutes of coughing, sneezing, and gagging, he was able to stand and reapproach the doorway.

Only darkness inside.

Instinct told him to turn around and not venture into whatever lay directly ahead of him. If he stayed in the courtyard until morning when there would be activity, and if he remained rational, surely someone would listen, and believe him, and take him to Adolfo.

But where are the rats? he asked himself. *Have they had enough to eat? Is it just a human trait to think that they are hunting me down, despite being satiated?*

He glanced up the alley, wondering if the ugly rodents were even then scampering along its length and would soon come into sight.

Then he saw the horde.

Perhaps it was a barely heard sound that alerted him, or some hint of the creatures' muskiness reaching his nostrils. Cyril saw the first few, not so much their shapes in the intensified darkness of that narrow alley, but those eyes, tiny demonic pinpoints, strange living rubies on black velvet.

The courtyard had a thick wall around it, roughly ten feet

high, made of a bricklike material. He could try to scale it but the rats, seeing him, and taunted by the smell of his sweat, would move fast then, far faster than he, and rodents were presumably better at climbing than a man who had done little over the past two decades. Besides, he had no idea what was on the other side. Or he could stand his ground, and try to fight them off—there were several chairs that, intact or broken apart, would serve as effective weapons—all the while screaming, with the hope that someone would be sleeping near an open window and hear him.

He had only one choice, given those two options.

Inside.

He would have to dash into the darkness behind him, not knowing what he would face, and yet nothing, he reasoned, could be as dangerous as the rats themselves.

Cyril backed up slowly. Even this slight movement on his part seemed to signal something drastic to them.

A chittering sound. . .

It arose from the collective mass of creatures, and they moved almost like a field of wheat with a strong wind rippling through it.

Cyril turned and ran into the darkness. As his feet touched the fallen door, he hesitated.

Lift it up somehow? he asked himself. *Block the entrance?*

But the door was exceptionally heavy. And what would he use to keep it in place while he continued running?

A shaft of moonlight illuminated a sliver of the world beyond the door. He saw coffins, not elaborate, hand-carved ones as back in England, like his father's, but simple wooden boxes. And there were black urns on wooden shelves set into the rock walls on either side, along with the remains of human body after body! Bodies that looked more like four thousand-year-old mummies from an Egyptian tomb, leathery skin, empty eye sockets, rotten teeth where there were any at all, the remnants of exquisite silks and linens wrapped around each one. And behind him. . .the rats. He sensed their presence, heard their claws scratching over the old wood of that door.

Closer.

Red-eyed demons with long hairless tails.

Foolishly, he had stopped for a moment or two to look at his surroundings and that had allowed the rats to close the distance between him and them. He started to run faster than he thought he knew how.

Then, suddenly, he was falling. . .

He plunged into what seemed like an abyss until he finally hit bottom, a softer landing than he had feared, centuries of dust acting as a cushion of sorts.

Shapes.

Man-made shapes.

Cyril saw around him the faint shapes of what looked like deserted buildings. And he seemed to be on a narrow street between them.

Where are the rats now? his mind screamed in heart-clutching panic. *Where—?*

Above him.

He glanced upward.

On the ledge above!

Cyril saw them looking down, trying to figure out some way to get at him. Ingeniously, the rodents proceeded along a tiny trail, until they reached from where he had fallen to what seemed the street below.

Cyril tried to move but could not. They were quick, these rats, circling around his body. He knew this, even in the darkness, because of their eyes, their riveting eyes, now transfixed on him. He could feel their broomlike fur on his hands, could feel their weight, not so much individually, but the collective press of them on his stomach and his chest. And their tongues, their wet tongues tasting him. One raised up to its full length. On his chin! As it stood there, it seemed to be studying his eyes while licking its lips. Even in the darkness, Cyril could see the outline of its teeth, so close to him. Sharp teeth. Teeth now closing on his helpless flesh, pinching it, pain lacing through his right cheek, the taste of salty liquid dripping over onto his tongue.

Another jumped up on his forehead.

Not my eyes! his mind screamed. *Not my eyes!*

This rat seemed fascinated by his mouth. It crawled onto his nose and then reached out and toyed with his lips, grabbing them, prying them apart. He opened his mouth slightly, not wanting to force the rat to tear his lips apart. Both rats were transfixed by the sight of his teeth, so completely different in shape and number from their own.

Tapping. . .

One of the rats started tapping a claw on his front teeth, gently at first, then more roughly. Cyril felt certain that they would invade his mouth and take his tongue and—

A sound. A musical sound! He thought for an instant that he was either going mad in the darkness of that unknown place, or that he had heard heaven opening up and the first music of an angel reaching his ears. Not heaven. Not heaven at all. The sound of an earthly flute. From some spot near him. So near that he did not have to strain to hear the instrument's ethereal tones.

A flute's song to which the rats reacted by leaving him after taking but a few seconds to recognize it.

Except the one on his chin.

This rat hesitated, perhaps tempted to take one quick bite before scampering off, but seemingly thought better of it, and soon rejoined the others. In a short while, the horde was gone, with only that strange melancholy song left as it played its way through his mind. Then the flute's lilting tones stopped, and a rich, commanding voice filled that ancient street.

"I am Baldasarre Gervasio," the voice proclaimed. "What are you doing here in my kingdom?"

CHAPTER 7

"You have broken nothing. And you will not feel much pain," Gervasio told him almost soothingly.

He was right.

Cyril was able to stand without difficulty and found just a couple of areas in his body where he felt some aches, which surprised him, despite Gervasio's assurances.

"I have heard a great deal about you," Cyril began. "And I have just seen how you are working with abused and under-privileged children, getting them accustomed to using computers."

"And I have learned more than a little bit about you, Lord Fothergill," came the other man's reply, that magnificent voice making even such simple words sound like pronouncements from Mount Sinai.

"You seem to think of me as some extraordinary model of Christian integrity."

"And you must consider me some symbol of evil."

"Not I only, not I only."

"That saddens me."

"That people see you for what you are? That you are not as clever as you hoped in disguising your true allegiance?"

"But you assume I am what they think. We all are strangers to you. Must you judge the right and the wrong so quickly, and at risk of miscalculating, especially when you should not be judging me at all?"

"Wrong!" Cyril exclaimed. "The Word of God says, 'By their fruits, ye shall know them.' What I think of you is not a judgment at all, it is a reading of the facts."

"And what are those facts, as you claim them?"

"That you are trying to undermine the Catholic Church, that you threaten to hasten its decline, that you are ruthless beyond redemption, and that you are in league with the Muslims to bring Europe to its knees, or worse."

"Is that all, Lord Fothergill?"

"I think you may be possessed, Baldasarre Gervasio."

Silence reigned for a minute or two.

"You think this but do not know it?" Gervasio went on.

"I leave open another possibility."

"What would that be?"

"That you are merely mad but hardly less dangerous."

Footsteps. The sound of footsteps. Nearby. And someone coughing.

"I am bedeviled by a weak throat," Gervasio said hoarsely. "This dust, the very air down here. . ."

"I would like to see you," Cyril said.

"You do not speak correctly, Lord Fothergill. You would not like to see me but rather, you are *curious* to see me. I am hardly the handsome fellow you are, nor am I at all like your dashing traveling companion, Lord Geoffrey Cowlishaw. Now there is someone the ladies must fight over, instead of me, from whom they always have run."

Despite himself, Cyril felt some pity for the man, but also greater apprehension, since he knew that years of emotional suffering could drive a person to extremes.

"God has afflicted me with a strange body!" declared Gervasio. "Should there be any surprise that I have spent the years of my life—"

He cut himself off.

"Seeking the dismantling of His established church?" Cyril probed. "Is that not what you were about to say? And while

I am at it, what purpose does the Internet serve in your scheme?"

"Think what you please."

"I want to see you face-to-face," Cyril pressed.

"So that you can spit in mine?"

"You deserve far more than that. Your henchmen have murdered several Vatican guards and—"

"Where is your proof?"

"Who else has a motive?"

"Why do you assume the motive is mine?"

"It cannot be Adolfo's."

"How can you know that, Lord Fothergill? Perhaps I am the hero here, not the holy father. Have you considered that?"

Cyril shook his head.

"I think he is weak and deceived, and you are evil."

"Are you wise telling me that, if what you say is true? Does not evil react violently when recognized?"

Seconds passed.

"And yet I am calm. How evil can I be?"

"Satan and his demons can don many disguises!"

"Including, centuries ago, those of knights in shining armor who mocked their image of valor by their filthy acts of pillaging and rape? Who is more evil? Those barbarians riding under the guise of being noble Christians? Or I who am merely dedicated to survival. . .my own, I might add."

"What about the plague?"

Cyril could hear Gervasio gasp despite himself.

"You sound surprised that I know. Is wiping out millions merely an act of survival, or a mad, obscene rampage of vengeance?"

Cyril smiled slightly.

"You are obviously more than any average man and something less than that at the same time. Others find your intellect fascinating, perhaps thrilling, if they are near you and catch glimpses of it as though it were something physical. But they must look beyond your body, and grit their teeth in the process."

"Am I not to be admired if I can survive all that, given my physical liabilities?" Gervasio opined.

"In a bizarre way, I suppose that is true. But you need, I think, not only to forge your own survival but you also find yourself compelled to dominate others.

"If you can exercise great power, you reduce the chances that anyone will stand up to you, that anyone will resist you. They can feel revulsion in your presence but if there is also fear in their hearts, then their disgust does not matter."

Cyril's eyes were getting used to the darkness. He could see ahead of him a shape, a shape quite small and slightly hunched over.

"It always matters!" Gervasio exclaimed. "I know that they laugh at me as soon as I leave a room. They have no respect for me. It is only the rewards and the punishment and the control that I dispense that keeps them in line."

His voice trembled briefly.

"If I were capable of none of this, they would stick a rod up my behind and roast me over a fire, laughing as I died in great agony."

Cyril stepped forward a few inches.

"Is that what you are most afraid of?" he asked. "Being burned to death?"

He heard Gervasio moving around, obviously discomforted.

"Do unto others before others can inflict terrible things upon you?" Cyril added. "Is that not your guiding philosophy? Accordingly, it matters little if you have to consort with a group of scum in order to strengthen your position."

"Business. . .Vatican business."

"What could the church ever have to discuss with heathens?"

"You are narrow-minded," Gervasio retorted.

"Then so be it. Are not the Gospels narrow-minded? They say, individually and collectively, that only Christians are to enter the kingdom of heaven, and no one else!"

"You make Christianity seem so intolerant."

"And your Muslim cohorts seem less so?"

"You have never studied Islam."

Cyril took that as a challenge, glad that Gervasio had given him the opening.

"Your assumption is incorrect," he said, relishing the opportunity.

"You speak foolishness out of ignorance," the rat man countered.

"You are the ignorant one, Baldasarre Gervasio. Islam demands harsh treatment of all infidels. They are to be 'slaughtered, or crucified, or their hands and feet shall alternately be struck off, or they shall be banished from the land.' Those words are verbatim from the Koran. And I have not even touched upon Islamic rejection of the Resurrection of Christ and much more that we all hold dear to our souls."

"I admire your considerable knowledge, Lord Fothergill," Gervasio replied, his tone chilly.

Cyril's lips curled up into a smirk.

"I understand that that is not all that happens to fascinate you about me."

"I have learned much about you."

"From my father, right?"

"Yes. . ."

"You wonder how it is possible that I can be what I am supposed to be. You have never met someone described to you as I was by my father. Certainly Raymond Fothergill was not talking about himself."

He regretted saying that as soon as the words left his mouth. Any sense of lingering shame over his father's lifestyle had been completely forgiven.

But Gervasio did not let it pass.

"Raymond confessed to me how much your indifference to him had hurt him over the years," he said. "He knew that you were ashamed, and he carried this with him as though it were a dagger plunged into his heart."

Cyril winced, knowing what the little man was doing but feeling too vulnerable momentarily to do anything about it.

"I had quite the opposite nightmare to face not very long after I was born," Gervasio told him. "I was never a cute baby, Lord Fothergill, never! My eyes were always too small, my nose too sharp, my mouth too narrow, my back, though hardly hunchbacked, was never straight like that of other children."

He sighed loudly.

"I was never attractive to any of the ladies. I was never attractive to any of the men. I had my own world, and I closed it around me, filled with nothing but what I conjured up from my own imagination.

"That was why I entered the priesthood, you know. I thought in serving others that I could somehow forget about this mediocre body of mine. I thought I could earn the respect, the friendship, the love of others by denying myself and serving them.

"It worked for a while, Lord Fothergill. People seemed to light up when I approached them. They would put their arms around me and greet me warmly. We would laugh together, we would cry together, I would hold them as they convulsed with pain. And I would be with more than a few when they died!"

Cyril heard Gervasio slur a few words, then clear his throat and continue.

"I thought that they were accepting me. I thought that, in doing the work of the Lord, serving Him with my mind, body, and soul, that the happiness I was at last feeling was surely one of His rewards for my service.

"But then I was late with some food for one particular family. As I walked up to their front door, I overheard them insulting me, referring to my poor physical condition.

"I was committed not to let that moment poison my thoughts. So I knocked on the door and they welcomed me in, full of smiles and pleasantness.

"I determined to find out if they were simply cruel exceptions. When I was deliberately late with food for other families, I came up against the same behind-my-back mocking, ridicule, sarcasm, thrown at me like knives. They cared not for me. They cared only for what I would bring to fill their stomachs."

"And so, as far as you were concerned, everything from that moment on was with revenge in mind?" Cyril asked.

"Against people, yes, oh, yes, but especially against God! I would be the one who exposed the hypocrisies of the church to the entire civilized world. And now that I have the Internet to command, I can plant seeds of heresy and blasphemy and disintegration all over the world."

He chuckled cruelly as he added, "I can do whatever I want. I can even bring together a group of people and have them commit suicide if I wish. Or I could order them to murder government officials. Or destroy country after country with plague!"

Cyril grimaced at the imagined scene that occupied his mind.

"The demonic specter of rotting corpses strewn across the landscape matters little to someone like you."

"There is no 'if' about it. Plague is the best way, Lord Fothergill. We shall start it in China, and have it move on from there to the boot of Europe."

The ignoble experiment of the Muslims and Gervasio united by a blood lust rooted in revenge would have Italy as the next step. If they were successful there, the unholy war would be unleashed upon the entire continent of Europe.

"And just in case something goes wrong, just in case your epidemic sputters and seems in danger of dying out before it reaches beyond Italy, you will infect many more of your trained rats and let them loose. . .not to mention helpless beggars."

"Now I know why your father was so proud of you."

"Raymond Fothergill at his most obscene was a moral and spiritual giant in comparison to a creature such as yourself. My father recognized that his drinking, his whoring, his wantonness were sinful, and he fought against those impulses."

Cyril's anger was mounting.

"You embrace your sins and seek comfort from multiplying them," he continued, his voice louder. "My father sought to do only that which was good and noble and kind, losing the battle more often than he won but still trying, still asking for forgiveness so that he could go on and fight yet another battle another day."

Gervasio clapped once.

"A very good performance," he said with exaggerated sarcasm. "But it assumes rather crassly that I have never wanted to change my circumstances or myself, that I have been interested only in causing the spread of disruption, pain, and death."

"You are conspiring with others to wipe out every man, woman, and child in Europe. That does more than *imply* your dedication to, as you put it, disruption, pain, and death."

"Do you honestly think that I or any man could walk through village after village with decomposing corpses piled in the streets and alleys, in doorways and hanging halfway out of windows, and not be affected?"

"Men with no conscience are able. Men possessed are able. Demons posing as angels of light are able."

"And, therefore, I must be one of the three?"

"How could I think otherwise, given the circumstances?"

Cyril could hear footsteps, not heavy ones, but more like the patter-patter of a child, muffled a bit by the dust of that place.

A candle.

He saw a candle suddenly being lit directly ahead of him.

"Follow me," Baldasarre Gervasio told him.

"How can I trust you," he asked, "knowing what I do?"

"You have an alternative?"

Cyril knew that he did not. There was no rational possibility that he could find his way through wherever he was and get back outside, either without injuring himself or having to face a ravenous horde of rats again.

"For the moment it seems that I have none," he admitted, hating the powerlessness of his situation.

"Moments down here can be long ones, very long for some. . ." Gervasio said in an intentionally cryptic tone.

Cyril saw the faint outline of a skeleton leaning against

one of the old rock walls. Sitting on top of the skull was a particularly large rat, its jaws moving rapidly, its cheeks puffed out from whatever food it had temporarily stored there.

"Pay that one no mind," Gervasio remarked with a casual air. "He would kill you only if I commanded it."

CHAPTER 8

Candles. . .arranged on three sides around an unknown object. . .

The orange-red flickering light made it possible for Cyril to see at least a few feet ahead in the subterranean darkness.

There was a simple box with a frame of aging wood and a surface of leather stretched over it.

Not a fancy piece of work, unlike anything that Cyril himself would have commissioned from a notable leather craftsman, the surface had only a single image engraved on it—that of a near-naked man crucified upside down.

"Are you not at least somewhat curious about what is inside?" Gervasio asked him from a short distance away.

. . . .a near-naked man crucified upside down.

That image suggested something that Cyril knew he would not immediately be able to deal with, no matter how much it tantalized him.

"Yes. . ." he replied, his palms slippery. "I cannot deceive you. Nor will I try."

"A man without dissemblance. How remarkable!"

"But is that not what you expected? Part of what you found so intriguing about me as you and my father talked?"

The reasons for Gervasio's fascination remained formless, with only Cyril's speculation to give them any kind of shape if not substance.

He wanted some kind of pronouncement from Gervasio about this but he did not get it.

"You may be right," the other man said. "In the meantime,

open it. Find out."

Cyril hesitated, half-deciding not to have anything to do with the box and to make a run for it, regardless of the consequences. As long as he remained in the catacombs, he was in a domain that Gervasio knew all too well.

The box itself was mundane enough, judging by a scarred and worn exterior affected by the passage of centuries. But inside, he might encounter something unknown to him, perhaps something quite dangerous.

Snakes or poisonous spiders!

"This is nothing more than some nefarious trap that you have cleverly set for me," Cyril said simply. "Why would I risk falling into it, and give you the satisfaction of standing by and gloating as I perished?"

In the darkness he could not see that the other man was smiling crookedly.

"Because, as a Christian," Gervasio suggested, "you have to be interested in the contents, my dear Lord Fothergill."

"Some old scrolls perhaps? Alas, I read only a little Latin. Such would be meaningless to me."

"More than that certainly. The Vatican has acres of old scrolls and various other parchments, some of great importance, but many just meaningless trifles. What you will find inside that battered box transcends everything else."

Cyril's pulse was quickening, as much out of curiosity as fear of what might be inside the box.

"Open it," Gervasio said.

Reluctantly, Cyril closed his fingers around the dry, brittle leather and slowly lifted the lid.

Lord, if I die soon, let it not be a prolonged business, he prayed silently. *I am not able to endure much pain without embarrassing You by my screams.*

He started breathing again when he saw the contents.

Bones.

As soon as the box was open, he saw a pile of bones inside, obviously old specimens, white-gray dust clinging to them.

"Be careful," urged Gervasio. "What you have before you is very important to the church."

Cyril picked up a portion of one arm bone and examined it.

"Amazing, is it not?" that voice pronounced, with a touch of awe. "The body of Peter the Apostle. . .and you are holding what is left of one of his arms!"

Cyril gasped and fumbled the single bone, nearly dropping it.

"In that one simple box you can find a fragment of St. Peter's cranium, one from his clavicle, another from his ulna, and yet another from his humerus. You will also discover metacarpals from his left hand, fragments from the pelvis and sacrum, and larger pieces of the right and left femurs."

Gervasio seemed to take delight in trying to impress Cyril with his knowledge.

"There is so very much more down here," he went on, "more than anybody has imagined. Above us, they fiddle and poke and, apart from Peter's bones, they have no idea what is here. I stand in the midst of all this and I feel secure. There is nothing but death here, Lord Fothergill, for what is history but the remains of what was once vibrant, once full of life, now dead. . .dead bodies, dead societies, dead dreams?"

Cyril put the bone carefully back into the box.

"But history can also serve to document that from which the Body of Christ has sprung," he ventured. "It allows us to catch a glimpse of the utter purity of the early church, and rejoice at the simplicity of worship in the name of Christ that the first-century Christians pursued, sacrificing their lives if need be.

"Do you really want to throw everything away, Monsignor Gervasio? Consider this: Would it not be better to change what is wrong and rebuild, rather than annihilate everything that has been accomplished, the wheat and the chaff consumed together?"

Baldasarre Gervasio snorted at the prospect, his contempt so strong that it seemed nearly palpable.

"I see mostly the hypocrisy!" He spewed out the words, and Cyril thought that he could detect some plaintive quality in the other's voice. "I see those foreign dignitaries fawning ever so conspicuously over the holy father."

Gervasio spat upon the ground, stirring up a tiny cloud of dust.

"What I found is that they are not interested in anything that is at all spiritual, most of them, anyway," he recalled. "The whole miserable lot. . .they want only their own degree of political advantage, nothing more, and they will travel whatever great distances are necessary in order to grab it.

"Their greatest desire is only to boast that they managed to get some time with his Holiness, and then exaggerate what it was that he told them. The holy father is not in the habit of handing out favors capriciously, and so the truth is hardly what they pretend."

Gervasio then muttered briefly to himself, but Cyril could not overhear what he was saying.

"I think not of what the church has accomplished," the little man continued more clearly, "but how far it has fallen from the early glory of centuries ago."

His voice trembled just enough to make Cyril suspect that Gervasio was having to fight back tears.

"Many of the men around his Holiness have been conducting business about which he knows nothing."

"What sort of business?"

"They sell blessings, you know. They get Christ's vicar quite innocently to bless endless numbers of bottles of water, items of clothing, crucifixes, and stones from the tomb of Jesus, having convinced him that the proceeds will be distributed to the poor and the sick and the dying in and around Rome, yet that is not it at all."

"But Adolfo could not know," Cyril offered. "If he did, he would end it all!"

Gervasio could not hide how saddened he was by what he had seen during the past two years of his service at the heart of the Roman Catholic Church, or his frustration at being unable to do anything about the spiritual condition of many of the Vatican's insiders.

"These men have profited greatly from the holy father's willingness to trust in their decency, and the church gets little of the money, while the homeless and the starving and the dying go on their way to some common grave."

"I find that as ugly and shameful as you," Cyril told him. "These men are the new money changers, and someday they surely will be thrown out again. But I beg you to consider something else."

"Tell me. . ." Gervasio spoke with something approaching genuine interest.

"The Protestant world is not free of this. We have 'Jesus loves me' ping-pong paddles and night-lights fashioned in a representation of Christ. We have cheap trinkets and bottled water from the Jordan or the Sea of Galilee. And there are the carnival-like TV evangelists, the so-called mass healings by men whose egos drive them on, not any real interest in alleviating suffering, men I despise."

"As much as you despise me?" asked Gervasio.

"You and they are dangerous, creating an impression of Christian worship that is more show-business entertainment than true worship or spirituality."

Gervasio was silent for a moment after listening to Cyril.

"When your father told me of you," he said, "I thought I might meet someday a truly honest man."

"But I am not perfect," Cyril responded. "I have sinned. I have been, on occasion, an embarrassment to a Holy God."

"Yet He surely does not turn from you in disgust as He must from me."

"Look at the Scriptures to which you have greater access than most men. He turns from no one if they accept His Son as Savior and Lord."

Silence.

"So close to the truth, and so far from it. . ." Gervasio spoke in a whisper, and Cyril had to strain to hear.

Something else. . .

He also thought he could detect what might have been a brief moment of sobbing before it was cut off.

"This dust continues to bother me," Gervasio remarked defensively, and Cyril did not challenge him. "But then I have always been tormented by one thing or another."

His anguish was apparent in the quiver that had crept into his voice.

"When I was younger, I wanted to die," Gervasio continued. "I had nothing but a deprived past. Even now, I would welcome death, you know."

"Do you have children?" Cyril asked. "Men who are fathers have a reason for living, and when they become aware that they are dying, they find some comfort in knowing that they leave new life, fresh life, young life behind as a legacy. That is what will help sustain me, I am sure."

Gervasio chuckled but without humor. "I have numerous children, you know, born out of wedlock, in country after country, but not a single one of them from love."

And he had no idea who they were or where they lived.

"I am the father of an anonymous multitude out there somewhere, Lord Fothergill," he said morosely. "I could be passing by any of those poor little ones at any given moment in the piazza or elsewhere and never know that it was so, never know that that one or that one or the one over there is mine.

"I should be holding every last one of them as their caring, protective father but I cannot, I cannot do something so simple, yet so divine, because they are no more than blurred faces passing me by. Even if I could find out, how could I ever present this wretchedness as their father? And there is something else, Lord Fothergill, something else that tears at my soul.

"For along with my appearance repulsing them, I would know that these young ones, these helpless little human beings came into this world not by any blissful act of sanctioned, ordained love but by simple lust, crude lust, forbidden lust, or worse. There was no other way for me. No one would willingly sleep with me. So I arranged for the kidnapping of any woman I wanted, impregnated each one, and tried to keep records but there were so many, all kinds of women from every walk of life, all carrying my offspring, all intimidated by my power into saying nothing, revealing nothing or they would be killed."

Gervasio used extraordinary self-control to say what he next did—

"Of my children, of my many children," Gervasio continued, "what number have been doomed to look like me, the only heritage from me some will ever have?"

It was undoubtedly a monumental task for him to continue, given the pain transparent in his voice.

"What number must see themselves as creatures when they look in a mirror or the water of a quiet lake and find their deformity reflected back at them? What number will someday end their lives by their own hands, unable to endure the torment?"

Cyril felt his pain.

Or was it all a lie, to gain sympathy, to—? he asked himself.

As though realizing that he had bared more of his soul than he intended, Gervasio's tone seemed to change, the fragile emotional display gone.

"Enough of that," Gervasio said, his voice a monotone. "Do let me tell you more about this place in which you find yourself."

Their way was now lit by rows of candles, lining each side of the narrow path that carried them deep into the catacombs.

"There are layers of tombs in this vast series of tunnels and caverns beyond even your well-educated imagination, some extending back to the second and third centuries.

"The faded frescoes are fascinating in themselves, some quite elaborate, others primitive, but all showing that people once lived here, lived and worked, with children playing in what passed for streets but which were mere walkways between tombs."

Cyril shivered at the notion that a man could elect to spend so much time in a place inhabited only by living rats, spiders, and other crawling creatures.

"So much here that pulls you back in time!" Gervasio proclaimed.

He seemed oddly enthusiastic, eager perhaps to spend the rest of his life in research among the tombs, unlike other men who made a pursuit of discovering lost remnants of history, only to leave and return to what was normal and healthy and full of life.

But not Baldasarre Gervasio. Not this man who would

never stand before his visitor and say, "Here I am, for what I am! Laugh or cry or shrink back in loathing but I will not hide any longer, I will not be ashamed for another moment. This is the way God made me, and I shall not let this form of mine force me into so strong a self-pity that the enemy of my soul gains easy entry."

Instead he talked and talked, his voice rising and failing.

"Two shrines to Constantine!" he cried with unbridled enthusiasm. "And, yes, yes, an underground chapel where, I suspect, persecuted Christians daily gathered to worship.

"And, beyond these, chamber after chamber yet unexplored, promising more discoveries, including, it is said, bloodstained pieces of the cross upon which Christ was crucified. . .these go on in every direction for distances no man can know."

Cyril saw the appeal of the pursuit and discovery of other finds, and his own instincts were stirred as a result but only as an avocation, not a lifelong sentence of solitary confinement.

"But this is a place of the dead," Cyril pointed out, "and you remain a flesh-and-blood man who yet breathes. Why do you spend so much time here of all places?

"What fellowship that is healthy can you have in this darkness? You need light, you need it before your physical eyes and you need it at the center of your troubled soul."

The other man sighed, but not with any contentment. It was a sigh of despair.

"It is more real to me than the land of the living. . ." he said, grunting. "Goodbye, Lord Fothergill. Find your way out. . .if you can."

And with that, Baldasarre Gervasio seemed to leave Cyril alone, alone to find his way out of a maze of crypts containing the faceless dead, people perhaps well-known and respected in their day, but now only part of the gathered dust and mustiness, the utter gloom.

Cyril thought he was doomed.

He had no idea what route to take. Going back the way he came seemed a simple enough answer, but even if he did make it to where he had fallen, he knew that reaching that same ledge, assuming he could even recognize it, would involve scaling the sides of one or more structures that were centuries old, and, in some cases, starting to crumble, heightening the possibility of injury or death.

But he had to take that chance, unless Baldasarre Gervasio decided to let him live, and he could have no reasonable hope of that.

So cold. . .

He had donned a warm coat for what he intended to be a few minutes in the piázza but here, in the catacombs, the chill air seemed far worse the farther he wandered, laughing in its own way at his attempts to keep warm.

He knew what was happening but could do little about it.

I am descending, he thought, going deeper into the earth. *And the farther I go, the less likely I will ever be found.*

Periodically he would see movement, red eyes observing him for a short while, then thin, bony feet carrying the rat away.

Waiting. . .

Cyril assumed that that was what the vile creatures were doing, waiting for him to become so weak that he would not be able to run away or put up little resistance.

Scouts. . .

He was convinced that the vast horde was waiting else-where, in subterranean territory known well enough to make it their own domain, the darkness no barrier to them, waiting for reports from the scouts, using whatever intelligence their rodent brains possessed to trap him ultimately and do their

grisly work. Such work could not have been just for the sake
of survival, since it seemed doubtful that Gervasio would let
his "pets" starve, unless he found hunger to be yet another
means of controlling them.

Suddenly he stopped walking.

Water.

How could that be? he asked himself. *This is land, solid
land, and there are no nearby streams that would provide—*

Yet he did hear something that sounded like water.

And he smelled it, smelled the dampness that it brought,
felt the cold wetness in the air.

Cyril turned north, then west, south, then east, trying to get
a fix on the source of that sound. His thoughts drifted back to
a time when he was sitting against a favorite large rock at the
northwestern end of his estate, facing Scotland, listening to a
stream in front of him, only a few feet beyond his legs, the
clear water flowing over stones beneath the surface of it.

Now he walked ahead a dozen feet or so.

He was closer, much closer to what seemed so like that
stream back in England, a sound that always lulled him to
sleep, though not like that this time, in caverns that could
claim his life. This time he could not allow himself anything
like sleep. To sleep was to die.

Water.

Rushing over stones and—

Then he felt it.

A drop. A drop of water. A drop of water from the rock
ceiling of the tunnel in which he now stood, hitting the top
of his head.

Cyril looked up toward the uneven surface of that rock
ceiling. Another drop touched his right eye and he blinked it
away. He walked forward. Dampness. More and more he felt
dampness. And cold. It was much colder, cold and wet. And

that sound, closer.

Then he saw it.

A stream, if not a traditional one, then something like it, water flowing from one end of that underground place to—

Flowing outside!

"Of course!" Cyril exclaimed out loud, the knowledge bringing him to a halt as he reasoned it out. "Caverns as deep as this, and in the midst of the rainy season, can—"

He snapped his fingers, realizing that he had come upon a possible escape.

"—fill up with water. Over time, soil and rock, no matter how tightly packed, are loosened, weakening the very foundation of St. Peter's. There has to be a conduit, presumably man-made, perhaps more than one, to take the overflow out to the Tiber."

He stopped, the danger apparent.

Snakes.

And spiders!

Cyril knew he could handle the possibility of snakes but not spiders, especially the tarantulas common to that region, since he had been bitten by one when he was a teenager, somehow surviving despite the most severe pain he had ever known.

Spiders. . .

Black, coal black, with spindly legs, eyes too large for the size of its body, that dreaded body covered with what seemed like stiff fur. Crawling over him, seeking the softest, warmest part, fangs ready to puncture him, venom rolling in an instant.

And when he was immobilized by their poison, helpless, but before he succumbed to a lingering death, it might be that the rats would chase the spiders away and, with some triumph, claim his still-warm body for themselves.

The conditions underground were right for all manner of creepy life-forms, the piles of bones long ago sucked dry amid patches of flesh turned dust evidence of their thriving populations.

And that darkness. . .

Total darkness wrapped itself around them to their pleasure since they so completely abhorred the light and skittered away whenever threatened by a visitor's candle.

Human eyes could only partially adjust but never penetrate that kind of brutal darkness, so much worse it was than what had terrified him when he was a child and yet oddly akin, oddly filled with similarly unknown things, imagined then but real now, very real. Such things could end his life, stifling his useless screams, while they filled his mouth and some fell down his throat, his heart protesting before it could no longer endure the shock without shutting down, and no one would know, no one could so much as guess what had happened to him.

A stream, if not a traditional one, then something like it, water flowing from one end of that underground place to—

He had to step forward, he had to follow that stream, had to face whatever might drop from a perch above his head and slither down his back, had to ignore everything but that flowing stream, which promised a kind of redemption if he did not give in to his fear and quit, dropping where he was, his courage evaporated as he simply waited for what must come, waited for them.

Deeper.

The water was above his ankles now. In minutes it was up to his knees.

Soon after that, it was deep enough to risk swimming whatever remained of its length. He knelt down in the water and then leaned forward, keeping just the bottom of his chin above the surface. For a little while, the current seemed to provide some momentum of its own but he still had to swim after a bit, still had to use his tired limbs. As he did, the very motion seemed curative and he got into the flow of it, the water now deep enough to drown him if he did not keep on moving.

Light. . .

Not far in front of him.

Could it be the moon? he asked himself. *Am I so close to the end of this nightmare? Will I soon see stars, blessed, blessed stars? And inhale fresh air once again?*

Not the moon. Not a steady ghostly light. Candles again, so many of them that the light seemed a living tapestry across the rock walls of that tunnel, a ballet of changing shapes and colors.

Cyril swam a little less frantically, the flow of the water itself taking over a bit more.

Just ahead.

An alcove in the sandstone wall of that tunnel, every available inch packed with candles, the odor of melting wax pungent. And a flat rock. A man sitting on it.

. . .short, about five feet, two inches in height, with thin shoulders, and he appears to have no neck at all, that bony face seemingly attached directly to his body. His arms are a bit long for the size of the rest of him, and he never seems to cut his fingernails as regularly as the other Vatican officials. He has a rather strange mustache, jutting straight out from his nose. . .like the whiskers of a rat. . .and his lips are narrow.

Looking like a bizarre, oversized rodent, his hair short but plentiful, his arms and legs bare, his skin pale, albino-like, the pearly pastiness evident in the candlelight.

And the eyes.

Tiny eyes. Tiny, bloodshot eyes.

For a moment, Cyril could not turn away, for their gaze grabbed him no less surely than a pair of strong hands.

"Nice of you to visit," Baldasarre Gervasio greeted him. "Sorry you have to leave, Lord Fothergill. My friends and I bid you a reluctant farewell. Under other circumstances, I could have enjoyed getting to know you intimately."

Hundreds of rats then swarmed over his body. . .on his lap, his shoulders, sitting atop his head, his folded arms, and on the rock floor at his feet. Restless rats, squirming, ready for a command, ready to do whatever their master bid them. And fat they were, these stealthy night creatures, their sides bulging from a recent meal, a juicy feast upon which they had gorged until full and then scurried back to the one who had sent them forth.

"That exquisite look of terror on your face betrays you!" Gervasio called out. "But you should not worry about me or my little soldiers this time. I need not kill a man who will soon be swept to his death."

And, then, those final words, muffled as Cyril was carried past, words fleetingly audible.

"Besides, there is just no room left in their tiny, tiny tummies."

Laughter, coarse, gloating.

"Lord Cowlishaw filled them nicely!"

Cyril screamed in shock and rage and a score of other emotions because of those final sadistic words issuing from the little rat man, words that echoed in his mind even as cool night air wafted against his face, a glimpse of stars welcome for but an instant while he was swept over the edge, dropping sharply, hitting a pile of rocks below seconds later, nerves protesting throughout his body before oblivion mercifully took him away from it all.